WORLD WAR II'S DEADLIEST ACES.
FOUR MEN AND ONE WOMAN, BATTLING
FOR THEIR LIVES AGAINST BOTH SIDES.

JOACHIM KOENIG (Englishman John King)—
Death-dealing commander of the squadron, personal friend of Goering. His love for the beautiful child-woman Simone threatens the safety of the entire squadron.

HANS RICHTER (Texan David Dean Smith)—Hard-drinking, boisterous, womanizer. Beneath his good-natured exterior, a man with a bitter vendetta.

ELSA DIETRICH (Boston blue blood Ginny Cabot)—Radio communications expert. A tall, blonde goddess willing to devote her very soul and body to the Allied cause.

FRITZ MUELLER (Australian Gavin Ingrams)—Young, hot-headed, impetuous. Obsessed with flying, but putty in the hands of a beautiful woman.

FRANZ VON SPIEGEL (Alexander Lyle Plunkett)—Eccentric, flamboyant, with a crazed lust for fighting.

THE DOUBLE CROSS SQUADRON

As passionate in love as they are ruthless in battle.

THE
DOUBLE CROSS
SQUADRON

William Parker Evans

BANTAM BOOKS
TORONTO · NEW YORK · LONDON · SYDNEY

THE DOUBLE CROSS SQUADRON
A Bantam Book / published by arrangement with
Book Creations, Inc.
Bantam edition / June 1982

Produced by Book Creations, Inc.
Executive Producer Lyle Kenyon Engel

ISBN 0-553-20668-0

Published simultaneously in the United States and Canada

PRINTED IN THE UNITED STATES OF AMERICA

0 9 8 7 6 5 4 3 2 1

Prologue

The outskirts of Hamburg, Germany; an August Sunday, 1938.

"Does the room please you, my dear?"

The large third-floor bedroom was adorned with polished wood, soft white linens and laces, all gleaming in the bright late afternoon sunshine; but the tall young woman in the tight-fitting riding habit hardly bothered to look at the expensive and tasteful furnishings.

"I do not feel the setting to be important, General, not at the moment," she said, and her voice combined the flawless diction of the German nobility with the satiny suggestiveness of a professional lady of the boudoir.

Entering the chamber behind her, Hermann Goering, Commander in Chief of the Third Reich Air Force, took in with feasting eyes the supple body of the woman before him. Again he wondered why he had never noticed her at previous social events. Such glowing black eyes. Such a sensuous turn of the lower lip. Such promise in the subtle movements of her hips.

He shook off that thought and closed the door. At such gatherings there were always so many women, and always it was he who quickly became the center of attention among them and among the ambitious men as well. Old and young had reason enough to honor and seek favor from the man who was, in fact, if not yet in name, the Fuehrer's first deputy. Not even a mind as sharp as his own could be expected to remember every fawning would-be courtier. But this one . . .

She turned to face him, and he moved toward her. It was perplexing that he could not attach a name to this inviting face and figure. Surely she must have been introduced to him—but, no, she had introduced herself, or rather, suddenly was there at his elbow as he was exchanging pleasantries with a group of officers in the garden. Was she the daughter of one of the senior officers present? A wife of one of them, perhaps. He was amused by that last thought. Her slim fingers he saw were ringless. But rings can easily disappear into pockets at convenient moments.

Ach, what did any of it matter? If some future arrangement were desirable, the details could always be managed easily enough. For this present, brief encounter, her name and family connections were unimportant.

"You are charming," Goering said softly. "Elegantly charming."

The half-smile that replied to his comment sent a tremor down his spinal cord.

"I can be more than charming, Herr General. But," and she moved against him, her fingers toying with the Iron Cross suspended at his collar, "not while we are both fully clothed."

Goering found himself swallowing hard. He also felt himself rousing within the tight crotch of his custom-tailored uniform.

"Er . . . yes. Yes," he said and licked his lips. "Shall we first, however, close out the distractions of the outside world?"

Goering drew himself away and strode to the long white curtains. Strange, but it was with a feeling of deep relief that, for the moment, he released himself from the deeply penetrating gaze of this fascinating woman's eyes.

2

Pausing a moment to view the groups of men and women chatting and drinking in the garden below, the officer pulled the fabric closed, muting both sunlight and the sounds of conversation.

He was surprised when he turned to face the woman.

"You look startled, Herr General. Am I displeasing?"

From her waist upward, she was no longer clothed. She was not in the least displeasing. He swallowed again and started to say just that, but she cut him off.

"Really, Herr General, I respectfully suggest we be somewhat quick about this. There is someone who shall miss me in the garden. Not that I care, but perhaps it would not be well to have everyone know the specifics of your own private afternoon pleasures."

As she spoke, she gracefully removed her shiny riding boots.

"Of course," Goering said and wondered why it was he felt like a schoolboy in the presence of this delightfully disarming and disrobing young beauty. Quickly, too quickly for a man of his great weight, he half-stumbled across the room toward the woman, who now sat on the edge of the huge bed. He cleared his throat again, stared at her, and fumbled uselessly at the leather belt holding back his flabby midsection. He sucked in and held his breath to relieve the pressure of his belt. Damn it! The buckle was stubborn. Well, a man of forty-six could not be expected to be built like a Greek Apollo. After all, his face was not unattractive, and his hair was still full. He grinned through his breathlessness and yanked at the buckle.

He explosively exhaled at the same moment as he freed the belt from its uncooperative buckle. Instinctively, his abdomen again pulled inward as he began to undo the buttons of his uniform jacket, all the while trying to hold the woman's dark and sultry eyes which never wavered from his own.

"Perhaps I might assist?" She stood before him now like some Botticelli Venus, a vision of beauty rising out of the discarded clothing at her feet. Totally nude, her skin

3

shone—no, glowed—in the light filtering through the closed curtains.

"I . . ." He got no further. His eyes were snapped from the consumption of female flesh toward the bedroom door. It was open.

The woman uttered a gasping scream, but she didn't matter now. What mattered was the man in the green uniform of the Wehrmacht—the regular army—who stood inside the open door. And what mattered even more was the heavy Mauser C96 pistol which was directed between Goering's frightened eyes.

"I . . ." Goering said again.

"You!" the man hissed, and his thin face flashed with murderous insanity. "You think because you are the big man, the great personality, that you can play the high baron —that you can treat others as nothing but serfs and can take whatever woman you choose, to satisfy your own filthy lust! You! The great Hermann Goering, you think you have the right to do this?"

The General's flaccid body strained to rise, but the wicked black hole at the end of the Mauser's barrel hypnotized him. "I . . ." he tried again, but once more his hoarse voice was cut off by the wild young man facing him.

"You have played your last cuckold game, swine! And now you are a dead man, Herr General!" The officer stepped farther into the room, his hand shaking with fury. Hermann Goering knew he faced death. And he was not ready to die.

"Nein!" he shouted, pleading, his bulky body dropping to the floor on its knees. "Nein . . ." he murmured, and his fingers laced themselves in supplication. His eyes fluttered closed.

It was over, all of it, all the promised glory. . . . The roaring crash of the gunshot filled his mind, and Goering fell to his face. The stench of gunpowder stabbed his nostrils.

Sound? Stench? How?

One eye glimmered open. Then the other.

No, he was not dead, not yet. But he dared not move.

Booted feet moved slowly toward him; he gripped his eyes tightly closed and tried to hold his breath.

"Get up, Herr General, quickly!" But it was the voice of another man. One eye opened cautiously. He followed the boots up to see a Luftwaffe Leutnant. "Quickly, Herr General, there is no time to lose!" Goering's eyes were open and he saw the tight face of a newcomer who held a Luger PO8. The General pushed himself heavily to his knees. Sweat flooded his face and body. His throat had no feeling. He could hardly speak. The Luftwaffe Leutnant went quickly to the door and closed it, then turned once more to Goering and said, "Your clothes—gather them, fast!"

Nearby on the carpet lay the unmoving form of the man who had promised Goering death. Crumpled, lifeless, the clawing fingers of his right hand were several safe inches away from the Mauser.

"I suggest you move swiftly, Herr General," the Leutnant said, and the steellike tone of the voice matched the straight carriage of the man himself. Goering, panting, and with ears still ringing from the gunshot, struggled to his feet. As if he were hypnotized, the General looked closely at the man who had saved his life.

The Leutnant was neat, trim, in his mid-thirties; and on his face was one distinguishing mark that could never be forgotten: a jagged red scar flashed upward from the bridge of his nose into the widow's peak of full, jet-black hair.

"Please, Herr General!" the Leutnant urged and pushed the Luftwaffe commander's jacket against his chest. "This can be fixed, but only if you get out of this room and off this estate as quickly as you can!"

The General looked at the woman, who sat unmoving on the bed, her face twisted by horror, her eyes fixed on the body lying on the carpet.

"And her?" Goering asked. "There shall be questions."

"There shall be answers, I assure you," was the reply. "Satisfactory answers, but only if you are not here."

"You? Why?"

The Luger seemed to shrug with the shoulders of the

tall man who held it. "I am Luftwaffe. You are Luftwaffe. It seemed only appropriate that your wing—your exposed wing—should be protected. But we have no time to speak now. You must go!"

The General bundled up his clothing, and his eyes stopped on the face of the immobile woman. "I'm sorry. I didn't mean to . . ."

The man with the Luger interrupted. "Do not bother yourself with dead women," he whispered. "The issue at hand is speed."

"You kill easily, Leutnant," Goering said quietly.

"When the honor and glory of the Third Reich, and particularly the Luftwaffe, require—I do, Herr General."

Goering looked again at the iron-set face. Yes, he remembered this man. Earlier today, champagne glass in hand, the General had wandered into a discussion of aerial tactics used in the deployment of German fighters in the recent Spanish Civil War. This young officer had made a good deal of sense, or so it had seemed before the swiveling hips in riding breeches took the General's attention away to more pressing matters.

"Your name, Leutnant?"

"Koenig, Herr General. Joachim Koenig."

"I shall not forget this debt I owe you, Koenig. Come to me in Berlin as soon as you can, and I shall see it is repaid."

"I shall obey your command, Herr General." Koenig bowed slightly and opened the door.

Goering stopped before leaving and said with a little smile, "It is not an order, Koenig. It is, under the circumstances, a request."

"Heil Hitler!" Koenig snapped to attention and gave the short, stiff-armed Nazi salute.

"Heil Hitler," Goering returned, squaring his shoulders. At the door he turned, and casting a fleeting glance at the man lying lifeless on the floor, he fled from the room.

"Do not move!" Joachim Koenig told the nude woman on the bed.

He stepped to the window and parted the curtains. He focused on a uniformed Luftwaffe officer lazily looking over the circular driveway of the estate's mansion. For three or four minutes the officer below stood there, then abruptly glanced up at the window, nodded twice, and turned leisurely away, as if in search of some more lively pastime.

Koenig also turned.

"The cats have gone," he said. "Time now for the mice to move out. Escape Route One is clear."

The woman began dressing. The man on the floor shoved her boots closer so she could reach them better. She grinned, sat up, and spoke to Koenig.

"And what shall I tell Uncle Freddy back home? Mission successful?"

The man with the scarred forehead holstered the Luger and nodded curtly. "Tell Uncle Freddy that Part A of Operation Eros has been a success."

In this Germanic setting, their words were strange, for they were spoken in very good Oxford English.

Chapter 1

9 June 1941

It was the beginning of a fine red dawn over the southern coast of England. The shoals of pink-tipped clouds soared up to the roof of the sky, but the two old men walking along the beach cared nothing about nature's heavenly dynamics. Their eyes were cast downward as they walked along the high-tide line, hunting, searching, scouring the oily sand for this morning's pickings.

One man was lean and tall; the other had long arms that made his stocky build resemble something earlier than man on the evolutionary chain. Both were dressed shabbily in loose-fitting trousers and shirts of grayish fabric which matched the nondescript cloth sacks they carried. They wore dark caps that once might have been green, and they needed shaves and baths. But their eyes were keen as they moved slowly forward and explored the beach.

The previous night had seen heavy action in this part of the English Channel known as E-Boat Alley. Instruments of all kinds, tools, boxes of food, clothing, and equipment—some of it still worn by water-soaked corpses—were to be found by the early riser and careful beachcomber. Things to sell, to use—even driftwood was good fuel in a time of war and rationing.

The Channel here in the southeast had blazed with light and roared with the sounds of destruction the night before. The warships of Churchill and Hitler had clashed on the water, and the airspace had screamed with battle, as well. Flight after flight of Jerry's twin-engine Junkers 88s, each carrying two tons of bombs, had zoomed in on London and its environs in one of the heaviest raids since the full-scale Battle of Britain had been called off by the Germans in mid-October of last year.

The two old men were sure they'd do well, but as of yet there was nothing in those gray cloth sacks; nothing had sent their old leather-shod feet scrambling along the tide line for booty.

And then, suddenly, something was wrong.

The taller man felt an itch under his cap at the back of his head. He scratched, and his eyes rose a moment from the sand and oily sludge to focus on the clouds in the southeast.

Two black dots were very low on the horizon, barely visible. Almost imperceptibly, they grew in size, coming in on a straight line, one dot slightly below the other.

"Harry . . ." the taller man said.

"Bloody scavenger!" muttered Harry as he spat at a seagull perched on a water-worn boulder some six or seven paces off.

The tall man's jaw dropped slightly. The itch was forgotten. The two dots were much larger now, and there was a soft, distant hum from their direction. A hum growing louder. They were coming in fast, they were.

And they were. Just under 350 miles an hour is very fast.

"Harry!"

"Lord's sake, Angus, what're you shouting for? No need to . . ."

Then Harry's eyes took in Angus's upturned face, and he looked in the same direction.

Low over the water, what had originally been dots

were now loud-buzzing bees with stiff horizontal wings. The first light of the sun blushed on the standard camouflage colors of dark green and gray.

"Messerschmitts!" Harry cried. "They'll hit us!"

"Us?" Angus said. Adolf's holy Luftwaffe wouldn't be after two old beachcombers. They were coming in low, obviously to avoid radar, and their target had to be inland. But, on that vacant beach, Harry and Angus would be easy potshots.

The drone was becoming a roar.

"The dirt!" Angus bleated.

Yanked by some master puppeteer, the two men flopped on their faces, but not into dirt. Not even into sand. They half-rolled, half-splashed themselves for safety into foul and oily sludge.

The two fighters screamed overhead with a deafening howl, passing just a few feet, it seemed, over Angus's contorted face.

Then, as quickly as they had come, lifting only slightly to clear the dunes, the planes vanished out of sight over the low fields beyond. The sound of their passing faded in the distance, but the ears of the two prone men still drummed with that sound as they cautiously got to their knees.

"C—close," stocky Harry said. "Too damned close, the Nazi bastards!"

"Funny," the taller man said, shaking sandy oil from his filthy empty sack.

"Funny? Sure, funny. I'll bet they're laughin' their bloody heads off," Harry spat grime from his crooked teeth.

"No," Angus said. "Not that kind of funny, mate. Strange funny, I meant. Them markin's under their wings —you see them?"

"If I had eyes in me arse I'd have seen them. With me kisser in the ooze?" The taste of sandy oil repelled Harry, and he wiped his face with a dirty, gritty sleeve that spread filth over his mouth. He snarled and shook his fist in the direction the fighters had flown.

Angus was on his feet, slowly shaking his head. "Aye, it was strange all the same. Under the wings, Harry. Where the single black crosses usually are—well, there were two crosses instead of one. And the same on the fuselage. Two crosses. A double cross, you might say. Strange."

But Harry wasn't listening. He was stamping through the sand, shaking the last of the muck from his sack and wondering whether he should take off his pants and drawers, too, for the grit had worked down his shirt into his drawers and was chafing him unmercifully.

"Two down, Major," crackled the light-hearted German voice in the earphones of the lead Messerschmitt pilot. "I assume they're upright by now, of course, and are probably calling us very unkind names. That I consider unfair, since I took their pictures for them. I think I'll title that one 'Home Guard Beach Defenses.'"

The leader did not respond. Behind his close-fitting goggles and under his flying headgear, his face was a mask of concentration. His altimeter registered zero feet. The air speed indicator quivered at the top end of the dial. The two planes flew close, the second somewhat above and behind the first in the classic "rotte" formation adopted by German fighters flying in pairs. The leader had full confidence in the ability of his partner and himself, but he wished the other —Hauptmann Hans Richter—would be less talkative, especially now that they were over English soil. Even though a Luftwaffe pilot might expect a certain laxness in British defenses this early in the morning—for there had been few dawn raids on England—there was always the danger that a stray radio conversation would be intercepted by ground units and reveal the presence of Messerschmitts flying below radar range.

The mud flats of the coast gave way swiftly to the checkered green fields of countryside. They were nearly at their first objective.

"Dowerston airfield four miles dead ahead," the leader radioed. "Cameras ready."

"Cameras ready," the Hauptmann—a rank equal to a British captain—in the second fighter replied.

"Two passes and then on to Target Two," said the leader. "Here we go. Let's go in, Hauptmann."

"*Hals und Beinbruch.*" Hauptmann Richter gave the salutation of "break your neck and legs"—the reverse good luck wish from one Luftwaffe ace to another—and the two aircraft dashed over the fields toward Dowerston.

Dowerston was one of the smallest fighter airfields in the southeast of England. Nestled in a green cup of lowland hills, the field was bounded to the north by a lake. It occurred to the leader—the Luftwaffe Major—that a castle on an island in the lake was where a minor Elizabethan poet had met his twelve-year-old mistress for secret dalliances.

So much for his English literary training, the Major thought. He pulled back on the yoke so the nose of his fighter climbed for higher elevation, and stabbed the button activating his aircraft's reconnaissance cameras. The Nazi high command's newsreel was beginning.

Dowerston had been the objective of heavy bombing the night before, and Goering himself had asked for film of the attack's effect. Still tightly maintaining the rotte formation, the fighters approached the complex of hangars, control towers and three runways lying as though asleep far below. A dozen Hurricanes and three Spitfires were drawn up before the hangars. Already, several steel-helmeted men were running like frantic ants, heading for the antiaircraft guns which were camouflaged here and there about the base.

But even before the gun crews reached their objectives, the cameras of the Me-109s had taken in as much of the north-south landscape as was necessary, and the planes were banking to the west for the cross run over the field.

"The film shall disappoint," the Major in the leading fighter said.

Below them, the signs of last night's attack were few, the only evidence of direct bomb hits being four circular interruptions in the smooth surface of the airstrips. True, the north end of the base border showed indications of charring and burning among the thick hedges of blackthorn and wild rose, but otherwise, Dowerston had the look of being serenely untouched by the war. At least it did until the antiaircraft guns began to speak, their fire erupting in black puffs of smoke around the fighters.

"Cut cameras," the Major said. "Time to move up and out."

Abruptly veering and climbing toward the north, the lead plane headed into a cloud bank. In a few seconds both German aircraft were through it. In ten more seconds they were above it, and the lethal bursts of ack-ack were far below them.

Hauptmann Richter in the rear Me-109 exhaled a long breath and rolled his shoulders to relieve them of their stiffness. The officer was six feet five inches tall and powerfully built. His body was always cramped in the small cockpit of the Messerschmitt, which was designed to carry the Perfect German. Unfortunately, the Hauptmann mused at such uncomfortable moments as these, the Most Perfect German was Hitler, who was not known for his towering stature. For Hauptmann Hans Richter, *Hals und Beinbruch* was more than a salutation—for him it was an apt expression with a painful meaning every time he flew long distances in an Me-109.

Fortunately, there was a source of temporary relief: the art of yoga. One could not, of course, twist into the full lotus position—particularly when one's nether parts were so deeply imbedded in the top of a parachute. But there were several yoga exercises which served well thousands of feet above the earth.

Richter drew his neck backward until the point of his chin touched his chest. He counted slowly to five. Then, sitting as erect as he could, he very slowly rolled his head to the extreme left. Again he counted slowly to five. Next, the backward bending position. Arching his back forward, he rolled his head to the rear of the cockpit and held it, satisfied and relaxed, for a five count. But as he began to roll his head to the right, his half-closed eyelids opened wide.

"Major!" he radioed quickly. "Four o'clock."

"I see them," the leader replied; they both looked to their right and downward—the four o'clock position of a clock's hour hand—and saw seven British Spitfires coming at them from the east, in formation like a swift airborne arrowhead.

"Damn!" The Major scowled and shifted his weight from one buttock to the other. Then he settled down. He experienced in that instant a total awareness of tearing across the blue sky in a machine of death. His fists were transformed from human hands into the controls of several Rheinmetall-Borsig MG 17 machine guns plus three twenty millimeter cannons—one on each wing and the third timed to fire through the 109's propeller.

As an extension of his feet, the Messerschmitt's powerful, liquid-cooled Daimler Benz twelve-cylinder engine pushed out slightly more than one thousand horsepower, and that was more than enough to send the two-ton aircraft on a mad 350-mile-an-hour dash to safety.

Unfortunately, the Spitfires closing from the west were Mk V-Bs, which meant they were powered by Rolls-Royce twelve-cylinder engines and had almost half again the horsepower of the German Messerschmitt. The heavier British fighter was twenty miles an hour faster than the current pride of the Luftwaffe—the Me-109. In a straight-line run, the Messerschmitts would not escape. But that wasn't the worst of it.

The worst of it was that the 109s had only enough fuel to escape by fleeing for the Channel to the southeast, and the Spitfires were drifting to the southeast, cutting off the sole escape route. And not only could the 109s be intercepted by the Spitfires if the German planes turned, but also the 109s were on a mission that would take them to the north where other British fighters could be alerted against them.

The Spits were closing rapidly now.

"We are boxed, Major," Richter radioed.

They heard the voices of the Tommy pilots who were

catching up from behind. Both 109s were at full throttle, but the gap between them and their British pursuers was less than one mile and narrowing.

"Shouldn't you say the magic word, Major?" Richter asked lightly. There was no immediate response. The rearview mirror of the Hauptmann's Messerschmitt revealed that the Spitfires were almost close enough to open up on the tails of the German planes. "You must have noticed that we've run out of clouds to slip into."

"I have noticed, Hauptmann," the Major replied.

The voices of the British pilots planning their division of the spoils came over their headsets. Then Richter spoke again. "With all due respect, Major, you must have observed that these Tommies are almost close enough to pluck my tail feathers."

"As you said, Hauptmann, we are boxed. Now, let's hope these particular Tommies have been duly instructed in the details of our special magic. If we ever needed a disappearing act, it's now."

The point of the Spitfire arrow loomed in the Major's rearview mirror. He adjusted his radio transmitter, but not before he saw a glitter of cannon fire erupt from the leading fighter.

In English—very good Oxford English—the Major spoke: "This is Nightingale, Spitfire leader. You are firing on Nightingale. I repeat, Spitfire leader, you are firing on Nightingale."

The Major could sense the spurt of cannon fire darting close to his aircraft. He radioed the message once again, this time with more urgency. Cannon fire rattled against his fighter, and he felt his blood rise in anger. Stupid bastards! He almost felt like opening up with his tail gun. He was surprised that the usually impetuous Hauptmann Richter had managed to restrain himself from doing the same. The Tommies on their tail seemed to be ignoring the message the Major was relaying, and they kept firing.

"I repeat! You are firing on Nightingale! Nightingale! Do you understand? Nightingale, hold your bloody fire! This is Nightingale!"

The firing stopped.

"Nightingale? Please repeat message." The rough Liverpool voice came over the airwaves from the Spitfire wing.

"Night-in-gale. Nightingale," said the Major, in a voice as crisp and authoritative as he could make it. "You are attacking Nightingale. Am I understood?"

The nine fighters hurled across the English skies, and the pilots in the aircraft behind the two Messerschmitts exchanged frustrated comments.

"Am I recognized?" the Major asked once more. "Repeat . . ."

"No need to repeat, Nightingale," the Liverpool voice came in. "You are recognized." A pause. "Welcome, Nightingale. Pleasure to meet you. You're talking with flight leader Jack Benn. And you are?"

A tightness came over the Major's face. "Nightingale, flight leader. Simply Nightingale. Now, if you'll be good enough to permit us to be on our way, we won't trouble your hunting anymore today."

"I thought you might want an escort."

"We're almost home, flight leader. In fact, I must switch radio frequencies now, so, thank you and farewell."

The seven-part arrowhead lifted and veered to the southeast. The two Messerschmitts barreled straight ahead. An exhale of relief preceded the English words that came over the Major's headset. It was Hauptmann Richter speaking, and the voice was more American than English.

"Every time we use that damned Nightingale routine, Major, I can't help thinking of Ernst."

In the Major's taut mind, Ernst Boch's Me-110 exploded in flames and fell into the English Channel. British Spitfires had caught him, but they did not recognize the "Nightingale" code name. Boch had been flying alone that March morning, and "Nightingale" had held nothing in the way of special magic. One of the two British Hurricane pilots who shot Boch down reported a strange communication from his victim, but it took some time before he learned the meaning of what had been radioed to him. By then it was too late for Ernst Boch.

"Did you hear me, Major?" Richter said, again in his American speech.

"I hear you," the Major replied in an Oxford accent. "But, at the moment, I'd prefer not to."

CHAPTER 2

9 June 1941

"Nightingale's coming in," the Luftwaffe Major radioed. He was now one hundred miles north of where the Spitfires had pulled away.

The response from the ground was immediate: "Come in, Nightingale. We've had word you were coming. You are cleared to land at once."

No doubt the fighter wing commander leading the Spitfires had cross-checked to verify that the two Messerschmitts claiming safe passage through English skies deserved it.

"I trust coffee is on," the Major said to the ground control.

"As usual," was the curt reply.

"Some new decoration, I see, Major," Hauptmann Richter said.

As the two Messerschmitt pilots in full flying suits walked toward one of four corrugated hangars arranged haphazardly about the small air base, Richter's eyes were directed to the left at a low-wing fighter with a fixed undercarriage and wooden two-bladed propeller. There were no markings on the plane.

"Polish," Richter said. "Panstwowe Kaklady Lotnicze

P.23B. Excellent ground attacker and fair tactical bomber. Unfortunately for the Poles, its capabilities never underwent real battle testing. The Krauts got them on the ground." The Hauptmann's English was very definitely American.

The two tall fliers walked past more than a dozen aircraft of various kinds clustered near one of the larger hangars. Most, like the two Me-109s that had just landed, were being serviced by anonymous men in olive drab coveralls with no insignia, rank, or unit identification visible.

Some aircraft bore national markings, however. Clearly identified were the red, white, and blue circles of France on a Morenai-Saulner 406 fighter and a two-engine Potex 630 light bomber. Two machines with Italian insignia were a Breda 65 and the small wooden SAIMAN 202, primarily a communications aircraft. The 202 was another new addition since Richter's previous visit of a month ago to this English airfield.

They walked directly to the central hangar of the complex. Except for the comments about the new aircraft, they had not spoken since landing—neither to each other nor to the men who had awaited them when they climbed down from the cockpits of the 109s. No greetings of any kind. No specific question or direction regarding the servicing and refueling of the German planes. Just the exchange of silent, unsmiling nods. Even the face of the normally easygoing Richter was unusually expressionless, as though he had stepped into a world of uncertain dreams. The men in overalls worked in a silence disturbed only by the occasional clink of metal against metal as tool met engine part.

The Luftwaffe pilots paused briefly at the personnel door to the central hangar. The exteriors of the four large metal buildings were identical except for the color of the doors. This door was blue. The man standing just to its right also wore blue, but of a darker hue. He was a large man, in his late thirties, about the same age as the tall Luftwaffe Major. But his frame was larger, and he weighed at least two hundred and twenty pounds, all of it hard muscle.

As the two pilots stopped before the door, the man in blue looked through them with unblinking eyes. Hauptmann Richter and Major Koenig stepped inside and, doing so, entered a different world.

The same silence prevailed here as outside, but now it was a silence with a ghostly quality. The place looked like something from another dimension—a dimension far removed from the reality of war. There were at least twenty gaming tables—roulette, wheels of fortune in several shapes and sizes, tables for cards and dice, ranging from sophisticated chemin de fer and baccarat to simple alleyway craps. The dominant color at table height was the green of felt, and that at boot level was the red of plush, thick carpeting. Overhead were four huge crystal chandeliers that, even in the room's dimness, sparkled as they turned on heavy gilded chains. The opposite wall was composed of bottles and glasses of every imaginable size and shape behind a polished wood and brass-appointed bar that ran almost the full length of the wall.

It looked as if the interior designer had blended together the most garish features of a Monte Carlo casino, a Hollywood-style wild West saloon, and a Victorian bordello for noblemen-only clientele.

The effect, in fact, was precisely what the interior designer had intended.

The two men stood silent in their inspection. The work on the casino room had not been completed at the time of their last visit. Richter tried to imagine what the place would look like when it was full of gamblers and used to its purpose, but the quiet grayness of the atmosphere kept the vision from coming.

The ghostly effect was broken off by a voice from an open door to the far left of the bar, a voice with an educated but somewhat frog-pitched English accent: "Coffee is on, gentlemen. As requested."

Inside the smaller room, the Hauptmann shook his head slightly at the coffee pot and the three cups at its side. "It was the Major who requested coffee, Colonel. For my part—"

"Yes, of course. Coming right up."

Richter nodded approvingly as a bottle of Jim Beam bourbon appeared next to the coffee pot. When a crystal goblet touched down slightly behind it, his face broke into a boyish grin, and he reached across the freshly waxed desk surface.

"Good to see you again, Colonel Standish."

"And to see you, David—well and in one piece —although I suspect you prefer the sight of the bourbon to me just now." They shook hands all around.

"You've put on a little weight, Freddy," Major Koenig said as their hands separated.

"My thyroid. Like other parts of my system, it refuses to take orders. Please, sit down, both of you."

The man acting as host, in his early fifties and standing about five feet five, was very thin. A few wisps of grayish brown hair covered what otherwise was a bald pate. He had a sunken chest and an almost nonexistent stomach. Thighs and legs hardly seemed to exist within the baggy flying suit he wore. Like all the military clothing on the base, his carried no rank or unit identification.

But Freddy Standish, Colonel, British Military Intelligence, was as hard as nails in will and in spirit. Those who knew him well, however, knew his will and spirit were surrounded by a bodily system that carried an unrelenting and slowly advancing malignancy that bit by bit was destroying the Colonel's life-support tissues. It was true, though, that in the several weeks since the three men had last been together in this room, he had gained a slight amount of weight. The observation of Major Koenig had a hopeful ring to it, but all three men knew the odds were already set—just as in the big gaming room outside—and they were tipped heavily against the Colonel.

"Please, gentlemen, make yourselves comfortable,"

21

Colonel Standish said. Both men nodded and sat down in the two chairs opposite their host in the sparsely decorated, windowless office. They removed their leather flying helmets. Richter scratched his short-cropped sandy hair, and Koenig ran his fingers through his own longer-cut jet-black hair. The confinement of Koenig's helmet had pressed the skin tightly to bone at the forehead so that it was almost white—all except for the scar that moved like a flash of red lightning downward from his widow's peak to a place just above the bridge of his nose.

"Well, John," Standish said as he poured coffee and Richter reached for the Jim Beam, "what has Goering's pet squadron brought the Reich's enemy today?"

Pet squadron. The Double Cross Staffel. That hadn't been the original idea when Freddy Standish decided to move one of his agent-pawns to centerboard in an attempt to create a listening post closer to the Commander in Chief of the Luftwaffe. The investment in the pawn itself had not been heavy, and it had been one that Standish had been politically eager to make. Looking across at the scarred Luftwaffe Major now, Freddy Standish remembered the unusually warm spring day eight years ago when he, then a lieutenant and in much better health, was summoned to the office of a very important member of His Majesty's Parliament.

Standish was told then that the MP had a nephew who required a new identity and a relocation. As it happened, he had certain qualifications that might make him useful to Standish, who was, at that moment, creating a special network of military operatives on the Continent—operatives who would be in place before the opening shots of the world war that Standish believed could not be avoided. Standish did not ask the MP if their conversation had the approval of political or military superiors. He silently read the contents of the thin file on the young man named John King as the MP patiently waited.

The young man who was the subject of the file had been brilliant in German literature at Oxford and spoke the language fluently. He was also a skilled pilot. The file contained little more of interest. "The—er, reason for his availability to Military Intelligence? It's not mentioned."

"I would rather not be too specific, unless I have to be, Lieutenant. A man was killed. A fight—the dead man's own fault, I am assured. My nephew can be—well, reckless at times."

"Recklessness has its merits in certain circumstances, sir. Will he obey orders, however?"

The member of Parliament smiled thinly. "Under current circumstances, he would appear to have little choice, wouldn't he?"

The wheels moved fast. There was an automobile accident, the apparent result of which was the death in flames of the MP's nephew, John King. The funeral was attended by a headline cast of dignitaries. Within a month a young man named Joachim Koenig registered at the University of Munich. Within three months he was accepted as a member of an amateur flying club. In March of 1935, when the existence of the Luftwaffe was officially recognized, Joachim Koenig declared himself eager to put on the uniform of Germany's flying warriors. For three years Freddy Standish gave little thought to the agent he'd created as a favor to a powerful politician.

Then came the idea for Operation Eros—and the selection of Luftwaffe Leutnant Koenig to become, as a result of the operation, a trusted confidant of Hermann Goering. Eros was a notable success; within two months, orders came for Leutnant Koenig to take up office duties in Berlin. The following year was heady for the Commander in Chief of the Luftwaffe—the planning and execution of the Poland blitzkrieg, further planning for the air strikes to come in Scandinavia, the Low Countries, France, and —when the Continent was secure to the Reich—England. The information that Koenig, by then a Hauptmann and a junior member of Goering's staff, was able to pass over the Channel was useful. But by the summer of 1940, with France in German hands and the Battle of Britain raging in earnest, Koenig's usefulness in Berlin had tapered off. The primary reason for that was that British Military Intelligence had scored another success, an outstanding one. Unknown to Koenig, and at that time to Standish, another spy had penetrated Goering's headquarters, one who carried the much more effective rank of Lieutenant Colonel. Standish received from his superiors a short message: "Can your Berlin man get himself moved to a more valuable post?"

By mid-September, Koenig had accomplished the job —and much more. Goering had been very understanding when the young man who had saved his life complained bitterly about being chained to a desk too far from the action. "Yes, you should be in a cockpit, Joachim, that is your rightful place," he had said. "It is just that I do not wish to lose your personal service to me." But Hauptmann Koenig suggested that such a personal loss would not be necessary.

Koenig suggested forming a special squadron with himself in command. Manned by agents selected by Koenig and whom Koenig could trust completely, the Staffel would report directly to the Reichsmarschall, and would fly reconnaissance as well as special missions of particular interest to Reichsmarschall Goering. For one thing, the squadron could give direct reports of Luftwaffe successes and failures against Britain. "Direct and *factual*," Koenig emphasized. "I doubt whether the mission reports we receive through normal organizational channels are complete in all details." The idea immediately appealed to Goering, who not only shared Koenig's uncertainty about the reports, but also was becoming suspicious that certain of his senior officers were plotting to place him in disfavor with the Füehrer.

Goering smiled. "I will miss having you in Berlin, Joachim, but I will give immediate authorization to command what you need. When your plan is complete, let me know—Herr Major."

Shortly after the beginning of the new year the special Staffel was in place. Three pilots were selected by Koenig from several candidates put forward by Standish. The ground crew was composed of faithful Germans with one exception: a special member of the ground staff who, courtesy of Uncle Freddy, was a radio expert posing as manager of the pilot's canteen on base.

As an immediate means of identifying the Staffel's aircraft to Goering—or to British and anti-Nazi agents when necessary—two military flying crosses were painted on the wings and fuselage instead of the Luftwaffe's usual single cross: thus, the name Double Cross Squadron, which also was designated by Roman numerals "XX."

The Double Cross Squadron. It was just under six months old and had already lost one of its original pilots, but its future looked promising.

A leather packet that the scarred Major Koenig had placed on the desk lay open, the papers in German and French spread so that the eyes of the Colonel, now behind thick spectacles, could scan them.

"These will require further study, John. Have you examined them?"

"No. Our friends in the French Resistance, the maquis, passed this package on to our contact. I only received it last night, and there was little time to discuss the contents with them. But they seem to think it of great importance."

Standish's eyes looked up from the documents and over the rims of the glasses; they met those of Koenig. "And how is she—your contact?"

"Still operating well, although perhaps not cautiously enough at times," the Major said.

Standish considered the reply thoughtfully, as if there were a variety of ways his question could have been answered. His slim shoulders shrugged as his hands gathered up the papers and replaced them in the leather packet. "Anything else?"

"Yes." Again it was Koenig who spoke. Hauptmann Richter seemed interested only in the Jim Beam—he was now silently sipping his second glass.

"Yes," the Major repeated. "As you know, our squadron's field is in occupied France, about four miles north of Lisieux in Normandy."

"Slightly less, if I recall correctly. Not much of a place."

"Except for the factories there. And especially, the factories to the south of the town."

Standish nodded. "Yes, the factories. I don't suppose our luck is such that you've come to tell me our French friends have managed to destroy them."

The pilot shook his head. "Still too well protected for that, but our friends the maquis have a philosophy—if you can't affect the output, you can try to work on the input."

"Meaning?"

"Meaning industrial diamonds. The maquis have gotten wind of a big shipment coming in soon and . . ."

Standish was suddenly on his feet. "John, you can grab these diamonds? You can bring them over to us?"

Richter looked over the rim of his bourbon glass and grinned. "There was, sir, a passing thought on our part that you might take a slight interest in that possibility."

"Slight interest? Good Lord, if you can steal these diamonds—"

"—some important Kraut drills and cutters that need them won't drill and cut," Richter completed the thought in his Western drawl. "Which in turn would mean that some Kraut plane engines and other machinery might not get built. Which then in turn—"

"To hell with the Hun's machinery! I'm talking about our own!" Colonel Standish paused to catch his breath. "Gentlemen, we need those diamonds. We need them desperately. We've got machines standing idle right now for lack of industrial diamonds! In the past few weeks, the shortage of diamonds for industrial use has been the damnable favorite topic of my superiors. Last month, our vessels bringing diamonds from South Africa were sunk, and the lack of diamonds is devastating our war effort! If it's at all possible to get this Hun supply . . ." He let the sentence trail off, waiting for some assurance from the other side of the desk.

"It won't be easy," Hauptmann Richter said flatly.

"What he means," Koenig said, "is that there are a lot of 'if's' involved. *If* we or the maquis can get the details of the diamond movement. That's one. Then, *if* a weakness in the security of the movement can be discovered in time to exploit it. Further, *if* the maquis will risk exploiting whatever opportunities they have—and, still further, *if* they can be persuaded to hand over the fruits of their labors to us—"

"They've been more than cooperative so far, John," Standish interrupted.

"With enough information, we might be able to do it. But we need to learn the secret code word, a code word that is used to control the movement of the diamonds. If we had it, we could send the shipment wherever we want it to go—into our hands—by using the code word at the right moment and to the right people. We need only precede the order with the code word, and the immediate supervisors of the shipment are compelled to obey our commands."

Standish listened intently. Koenig went on.

"Once the orders we choose are given, we'll have some time to cut off the truck carrying the diamonds before the Nazis realize they've been duped. But that is only *if* we can get that code word from the local SS man in charge of the shipment."

There was a lengthy pause. Then Standish spoke: "You and your people might have to be the operatives on this one, John."

"We're not guerrillas, Freddy. The risk in this—"

"There's no time to organize a special team. It's a risk you'll have—"

"The risk that one of us, alive or dead, will be recognized—that's what I was speaking of. What would happen to my squadron then—to its mission, to its tremendously valuable potential for the British war effort?"

The Colonel's face was grim. "If we can get those diamonds, John, it might be worth the trade-off," he said slowly.

Now it was Major Koenig who was on his feet, his red

scar flaring. He spoke flatly. "I'll decide the risks my squadron shall take, Colonel Standish."

"You will—" Crimson heat flashed over the British officer's face. "We happen to be talking about something that is vital—I repeat, vital—to our war effort. You . . ." And then the heat was gone, and Standish exhaled slowly. "You . . . shall do what you think is best to do, John. We both know that. It's just that sometimes priorities are difficult to weigh. I trust, however, you understand just how important these diamonds are."

The Major sat down. "I understand, Colonel. My apologies."

"No need for them. Now—a change of subject, if I may. What did you think of the casino out there?"

"Impressive. Expensive too, by the look of it."

"Very," the Colonel admitted.

"Worth it?"

"We'll know when we have to use it."

"And you feel we'll have to?"

"I want to. In any case, there's no way out of using it. You've already spoken to Goering about your discovery of a secret black market in England—an air base run by private enterprise where international espionage is traded."

"Not to mention," Richter put in, "certain delicacies that can be acquired, like Hermann's favorite brands of rare Scotch whiskeys. He has already expressed his enthusiasm with regard to that particular discovery."

"He has," the Major agreed. "But there's an argument for saying the Double Cross Staffel could continue to supply the Reichsmarschall with Scotch and false military secrets without creating the black market air base in the flesh."

The British officer nodded. "Perhaps we could, but sooner or later one of your German friends is going to want to see the place for himself. If one does—and if he is important enough to us—I want him here for a visit. I want him exposed to some of our fun and games, and to some of our people who, in a manner somewhat more pleasant than the German system, are expert at information extraction."

"Percival Bellows, for example," Richter said.

"For example, yes. Perhaps our best example, but not the only one. In any case, before you leave today, I want you to go through all the other hangars. The work is just about completed in them, and you should be fully familiar with the setup."

"Fine," Major Koenig said.

"Now, one more thing. Your Staffel's new man, Mueller, the replacement I told you about last month. Have you decided to accept him?"

"Yes, but I don't like his being Australian," Koeing said.

Standish grinned. "You didn't much care for Americans either, as I recall." He was looking at Hauptmann Richter as he spoke.

"Who's American?" Richter said, pouring more Jim Beam into his glass. "Where I come from, we call ourselves Texans." His drawl, for effect, was thicker than usual. "But I don't expect limeys to understand the obvious difference, Colonel."

CHAPTER 3

Tuesday, 10 June

It was 11:40 p.m. In the hazy light of a half-moon, the country estate north of Lisieux resembled an old house from the haunted pages of Charlotte Brontë. In the tree line overlooking the large house, a figure lay in the shadows, eyes watching for any movement.

There was none. There hadn't been for the full fifteen minutes since the figure had first silently taken up the post. There was no reason to expect movement at this hour, but there was real reason for caution. A little too much confidence could lead to carelessness. A careless act, no matter how small, could lead to death.

Because the tree line was west-northwest of the house, the position of vigil also afforded a clear view of the landscape to the south—clear when the air was clear, which tonight it was not. But, no matter. What the prone observer expected to see from that direction would not need any extraordinary clarity of vision.

Black-gloved fingers pushed back a dark cotton sleeve. 11:42, the watch said. Still no movement at the house, no indication of anything being other than what it should be.

Had the worst happened, the windows would be pouring light onto the high grass surrounding the house. Even if someone had commanded that the house be darkened in order to better catch a mouse in the field, one light would be on—a light in a second-story bedroom, a light positioned so that it could be seen only from one vantage point—the particular vantage point from which the seeking eyes in the shadows at the tree line watched.

11:43.

There was always the chance, of course, that he who had responsibility for switching on that upstairs light was prevented from doing so. A remote chance, to be sure, since it could be activated from six separate locations. But if he was prevented . . . if, for example, he was dead. . . .

11:44.

It was normal, the feeling of dread at this point. It was the waiting, the silent, still waiting that brought the feeling on. When moving, things were different. Then the mind was occupied with many variables—the need to move in silence, the need to take in and instantly analyze visual data that changed continually. But now, in this waiting phase, nothing moved, nothing changed.

11:45.

The sweep second hand of the watch had stuttered to a point midway between the five and six when there was a sudden lighting of the sky to the south. It was not a great flash, but in the grayish black gloom of the night it was reflected to look larger. It was a sudden flash like the lightning of a distant summer storm. And with the lightning came the deep boom of thunder. Just a single boom, then all was silent in the night once more, and the watching eyes returned to gaze at the house and its grassy landscape.

Five minutes went by, minutes in which no one inside the house ventured outside to investigate the cause of the thunder from the south. If unfriendly eyes had been within, they would have been watching all approaches, and at least one pair of eyes would have seen the curious flash. It would take a stern commander to keep his minions silent so that no sound whatever might come through the open windows to the outside. But there were such commanders, and that had to be recognized.

The figure rose to a low crouch.

With catlike movements, the dark form moved down to and through the high grass, parting it and keeping low within it, moving as if swimming toward the darkened house. If there had been an observer at the window, he would have seen only a slight rippling wavelike motion, as if a soft night wind had suddenly blown up, concentrating a continuous breath onto a once-immaculate lawn that had been left to overgrow. Nothing at all would be unusual in the sight, unless there were an observer, and unless the observer were looking for such a sign.

The observer waiting on the other side of the open window was, in fact, looking for such a sign. The 8mm pistol in the observer's right fist was cocked and ready.

It took less than nine minutes for the silent form to crawl through a space between the thick hedges surrounding the outer walls of the house and take up a position directly below the nearest window. The tension lasted for the length of four heartbeats.

The observer waiting in the room placed the pistol on an end table beside the chair in which his vigil had been kept. Then, he moved decisively and quickly to the windowsill. In the moonlight, his white hair shone and he was frail-looking. But his strides beneath the flowing striped nightshirt emphasized that this body, which had served for more than seventy years, was still hard and responsive, like the mind that guided it. He firmly took the hand extended upward to the window and, with a powerful heave, pulled the night stalker into the darkened room.

In the dimness the old man smiled at the other, who was built even more slightly than himself. With an exaggerated bow, he gestured toward the upstairs.

"Madame's bath awaits her," he said affectionately.

In the large, ornate porcelain tub, the mistress of the estate luxuriated in the warm soapy water. The cotton jacket and trousers, the black gloves and boots, the socks and light shoes she had worn into the house were now safely concealed in a section of wall under the wash basin. There was no use laundering them yet, for they would be needed again soon. Her body was another matter, as neither the dust and grime of the countryside nor the perspiration of overexertion was suitable to a woman of her station in life.

She was thirty-one years old, but she looked much younger. As she stepped from the tub and applied the large white towel to her pink flesh, her body exhibited the trim limbs, tiny waist, firm buttocks and small breasts of a teenager. Under the short black hair that bordered her oval face, large brown eyes conveyed the impression of innocent youth and inexperience. And there was something of Oriental femininity about her that added a certain sensuality—something about her bit-too-wide mouth, perhaps, or maybe it was the way the fine nose turned up at the end like a fairy tale pixie's.

Whatever it was, the mistress of the house—she was known by the unlikely name of Countess Wilhelmina von Coburg—was beautiful because she had it. But in these troubled days, that quality of beauty could not be seen by the eyes of the many young men of good taste who would have been most appreciative.

As she dried herself, she relished the touch of the soft towel against her thighs, her flat tummy, the nipples of her breasts. The dim light in the bathroom was enough for her to see her reflection in the full-length mirror that covered part of the wall near the doorway to the master bedroom. The mirror once had been the prized property of the late and presumably lamented Count Erich von Coburg. She had never met the gentleman who, thrown from a horse and killed in 1934, still lingered impotently in the house in the form of several silver-framed photographs. In the downstairs drawing room was a large oil portrait of the count, whose homely face had flaccid, hoglike jowls and a space between the two upper teeth that resembled an alley between two tall yellow buildings.

Involuntarily shuddering at the thought of such a beast

laying hands on her flesh, she wondered how the original and authentic Wilhelmina had ever endured it. And once again she wondered whether the real countess's wheelchair which was waiting in the next room, had been originally acquired to accommodate a physical ailment or to satisfy the wish to be left untouched by the count. It was a curiosity that probably never would be clarified. The real countess was being kept incommunicado and closely guarded—if indeed she still were alive—somewhere in England.

She shook off the morbid train of thought. There was enough in her own present circumstances to be morbid about if she wished. No, right now, let her warmed flesh delight in the movement of the soft white towel. . . .

"Madame is more narcissistic than usual this night," the male voice said from the dark of the bedroom—and in precisely clipped German.

The towel fluttered to the floor as the woman, with a cry of alarm, dove toward the small cabinet beside the mirror. Her left hand was on the catch when the man spoke again.

"You would never make it, you know. Before your fingers ever came close to touching the pistol, your lovely body would be riddled with bullets."

Her hand left the catch and she stood, both hands now moving up to straighten her hair. She smiled to herself at the automatic gesture that was a memory of when she'd had hair long enough to straighten. Her smile broadened as she walked through the doorway and into the darkened room.

He sat on the bed, fully dressed except that his boots were off and carefully placed upright next to her wheelchair. She realized that his position had given him a full view of herself the whole time she had been out of the tub.

"You are a real bastard sometimes," she said in French, snatching a towel, and feeling her cheeks suddenly flushing.

"Sometimes," Koenig replied, also in French.

She stopped at the foot of the bed, her eyes seeking

his in the dark. "You are also sometimes extremely incautious. No word came to me that you would visit tonight."

"I tried earlier. You were not at home. Attending the fireworks, I suppose?"

"Attending *to* them, yes."

He remained motionless on the bed. "Anything important?"

"No. A small warehouse, nothing significant in it. Just a reminder to the Boche that we maquis are still alive and well."

When he said nothing in reply, she continued, an edge to her voice. "And you—are you here for a reason? Other than that of playing voyeur, I mean."

Koenig stood and stepped to her, his frame towering above hers, but his eyes—eyes that she could now see clearly in the light of the bathroom behind her—showing that he admired her as an equal. Indeed they showed a trace of something else, something that neither of them could afford to give recognition to, not now and maybe not ever.

"The last time we spoke, you mentioned industrial diamonds," he said. "We want them."

She looked from his eyes to his face, all of it, including the forehead scar. She'd often wanted to ask him about that scar, how he had earned it. One day perhaps she would, but the time had never been right to do so.

She gave her head a hard shake. "*We?*"

"We," he said.

"Your people have said this to you?"

"Yesterday. I was across the Channel."

"You told them you would arrange the matter?"

"I told them nothing of the kind. I told them Simone would be asked to assist, that's all."

Simone smiled. "I may be asked, but there are others who will have to be persuaded. The maquis have their own priorities."

"That is true. But Simone could do the persuading, of that I have confidence."

"But could Simone be persuaded? Do you have confidence with regard to that?"

It was his turn to smile. "No. One can but try."

"Are you determined to try?"

"Very."

"Tonight? Now?" In spite of herself, she felt her heart beating with a sudden and expectant fury.

"Tonight. Now," he replied, and he took her gently to him, his arms holding her close.

"How long can you stay?" she asked quietly.

"As long as is necessary. As long as I possibly can."

As they moved toward the side of the bed, her fingers already were at the buttons of his jacket.

"Halten Sie!"

Half a dozen flashlights on both sides of the dirt track flashed on. The driver of the canvas-topped Volkswagen 82 braked and shoved the gearshift into neutral. He did not kill the motor.

The SS officer looked nervous as he approached the driver's side of the vehicle, and the result was that his dozen underlings, most of them armed with machine guns, looked even more edgy.

"Ah—Major! Heil Hitler!" the Leutnant shouted, saluting. Major Koenig returned the stiff-armed salute. "Heil Hitler!"

"Er, your identification, Major?"

Koenig's eyebrows furrowed under the vertical scar. "You don't recognize me?"

"Ja—Jawohl, Herr Major. But my orders are that I must examine the identification of all who . . ."

"Very well, Obersturmfuehrer." A compact leather wallet came from the Major's jacket and was extended to the SS officer who, in turn, opened it, closed it without examination and returned it. "Thank you, Obersturmfuehrer," Major Koenig said, returning the wallet to his pocket.

"Thank you, Herr Major, for understanding."

"May I proceed now?"

There was hesitation in the SS officer's reply. "I am

afraid, sir, that my orders are that I must request—I mean . . ."

"Please make yourself comprehensible, Obersturm-fuehrer. As you may have noticed, it is after three in the morning. I would very much like to get out of my uniform and into bed, if I make myself clear."

"More than clear, Herr Major! But I must ask you why it is you are away from your base this night. There has been an attack against one of our installations and . . ."

"Which installation?"

"It is not for me to say, Herr Major. Pardon, Herr Major, but I am ordered to ask . . ."

"Where I've been. Is that correct?"

"Yes, Herr Major. If you kindly will . . ."

"No."

Silence. Then: "No?"

"No. I assume you will make a report on your contact with me and what I said to you."

"But yes. I have no other choice, Herr Major."

The Major nodded. "I fully understand. Simply make your report, but make sure you quote me accurately."

"Quote you, sir?"

"Fully and accurately. I'm telling you it's no business of the SS whose bed I decide to share—especially in the middle of the premorning hours when I sincerely desire to occupy my own. Now, if you kindly will tell your men to get out of the road, I will attempt not to run any of them down. Heil Hitler!"

"Heil—men, move! Out of the Major's way!"

It was good, Koenig decided as his vehicle shot forward, that the Obersturmfuehrer's men appeared to have had some diving training in their youth.

Chapter 4

Feldwebel Heinrich Stumpf clicked his heels together. Since he weighed in at just under three hundred pounds, his heel-clicking, if ever executed with exactitude, would be heard by every ear in the squadron. Fortunately, the staff sergeant rarely was exact in such matters.

"Heil Hitler!" he bellowed.

"Heil Hitler," returned Major Joachim Koenig, but with considerably less enthusiasm. He remained seated, and his hand hardly reached the halfway point of his shoulder.

"You sent for me, Herr Major?"

"I did, Feldwebel Stumpf."

"Have I done something to displease you, Herr Major?"

"Have you, Feldwebel? Why don't you tell me?"

The staff sergeant straightened up as far as it was possible for him to do. His uniform was the largest size that the Luftwaffe ever had been called upon to supply; even so, his overall appearance was much like a badly-filled sack of grain.

"I can think of nothing serious, Herr Major," he said. "Of course, if the Major would possibly give me a small hint . . ."

"I will let you think about it, Feldwebel."

"As you say, sir. Er, now?"

"Not now. I want your opinion on something else."

The Feldwebel's eyes blinked. "The Herr Major wants my opinion?"

"I believe I said that. Did I not make myself clear?"

"Perfectly clear, sir!" Beads of sweat began to appear on the Feldwebel's brow. "Er, but the Herr Major did not say . . . well, I mean, it was not said what my opinion was wanted on. That is to say . . ."

"Feldwebel."

"Sir!"

"Will you kindly relax?"

"I—I am relaxed, Herr Major."

"Fine. Now if you will relax your trembling as well. If you stop holding your breath for lengthy periods, it might help you."

Air exploded from strained lungs. "Ah . . . I wish to thank the Herr Major for his suggestion." Inhale, exhale. "I would not have thought to—I mean, if it had not been for the suggestion of the Herr Major . . ."

"Feldwebel!"

"Herr Major!" The Feldwebel was stiff again.

"Please . . . don't shout."

"As you wish, Herr Major." Inhale, exhale. "It's not something to do with the aircraft, is it?"

"Why would I be asking you about the aircraft? Have you or your men been slacking in their service?"

"N—no! I allow no slacking, Herr Major. I assure you that our Staffel's planes are the most important things to me in the whole world!"

"More important than the men who fly them, Feldwebel?"

"The men? Nein, nein! Herr Major, the men are the most important people to me in the entire world! Er, next to my kind, loving old mother in Cloppenburg."

The Major's eyes narrowed. "I assume you have considered everyone?" He turned to examine a large framed photograph that hung on the wall behind the desk —a photograph of a pale-faced man with a lank cowlick of hair over his forehead and a toothbrush mustache.

"Oh. Well, I—I mean . . ."

"Of course, Feldwebel," the Major said, his eyes no longer slits, his voice without its previous edge. "I understand completely. Now, you said you have a special feeling for the men of this Staffel, is that correct?"

"Herr Major, I swear to you that I . . ."

"There's no need to swear to anything at all, Feldwebel. I only wish to know if that special feeling has extended itself to include our new young officer, Leutnant Mueller."

"The new Leutnant, Major?"

"Yes. I wish to know what you think of him."

The Feldwebel considered his words carefully, almost watching each one as it exited between teeth and lips. "He is—young, Herr Major."

"I know that. Twenty-five, to be precise." An eyebrow cocked. "But, wait—are you saying he's *too* young? Immature, perhaps?"

"Nein!" A deep inhale. "Nein, Herr Major, I was merely observing that he is young, that is all."

"What else have you observed?"

"He . . . dresses neatly, smartly in his uniform."

"What about his general attitude? How would you describe that?"

The huge man shifted his weight from his left foot to his right, then back again. "I—I am not good at describing in words, Herr Major."

"Try, Feldwebel. It isn't as though we haven't had similar talks before, you know."

The Feldwebel swallowed hard. How well he did know. He had been through the same thing six months before, when the Oberleutnant von Spiegel had first joined the Staffel. That had been a most difficult time of word choosing, since the Oberleutnant had certain mannerisms that were, well, different. Nonetheless, he was a good pilot and took care of his machine, and the Feldwebel knew that Major Koenig trusted von Spiegel completely.

"I'm waiting, Feldwebel."

"Er, yes. Well. Yes." Eyes rolled. "Well, there is a certain stiffness, sir," he said rapidly. "A stiffness of his body and also the way he talks to you that says he thinks he is superior like a member of the old nobility. Except . . ."

"Go on."

"Except, sir, that one suspects he is not a member of the old nobility but would like to be."

"And do you find this offensive? Or, rather, distasteful?"

A slight smile came over the plump face. "I do not think it will continue for long—not under the Herr Major's command."

Koenig nodded briefly. "Anything else, Feldwebel?"

"No, Herr Major."

"You wouldn't hold anything back?"

"No, Herr Major."

"Think about it carefully, Feldwebel. If I accept this Leutnant into our small Staffel, he will be piloting our aircraft—*your* aircraft."

"He—he appears to be a respecter of machines, Herr Major. I have seen him place his hands on my planes, sir. No, he will not abuse . . . what I mean is . . ."

"I understand. You think I can trust him with your beloved Messerschmitts. You think I should not reject the orders which send him to join our squadron."

The fat man's face was serious, his eyes lowered. "Herr Major, before being assigned to this Staffel, I worked elsewhere for the Reich, as you know. I observed many men of the Luftwaffe. Not all of them consider the machines they fly as their equal partners. This man seems to understand the aircraft. It *is* a good thing when a man feels that way." Pause. "I am not good with words, Herr Major."

"You do very well with words, Feldwebel. Very well. Now—if you will do me one small favor?"

"Of course, Herr Major."

"If you will kindly find the young noble, Leutnant Fritz Mueller, and request that he march his neatly pressed uniform to my office forthwith, I shall advise him as to my decision with regard to his membership in our small but select family of the Staffel of the Double Cross."

"Jawohl, Herr Major! Heil Hitler!"

As the Feldwebel executed an about-face and lurched through the doorway, the man behind the desk closed his eyes tightly. Softly, Feldwebel, he thought. For the sake of God Almighty and all his creatures, both in heaven and on earth—softly.

Still standing at attention after returning the fat Feldwebel's salute, Leutnant Fritz Mueller stared as Stumpf waddled back to work on his beloved planes.

So, Mueller thought. So now it comes, the time when the Herr Major Joachim Koenig, the great John King of British Military Intelligence, deigns to conduct his interview. Now comes the moment when His Mighty Lordship conveys to the unworthy servant his decision of acceptance or rejection. John King! The Koenig name better suited him—the man either was an accomplished actor with many years of training behind him or he had a natural personality that out-Germanned the damned Hun at his very worst!

Under his disguise as Luftwaffe Leutnant Fritz Mueller, Australian Gavin Ingrams was boiling in a hot fury. Since he'd been dropped off at the base this morning in the twin-engined Me-110c, he'd been treated exactly the opposite of the way he'd anticipated. You'd think they'd be happy to have somebody like himself on their side —somebody volunteering for duty in a unit that ran tremendous risks. His Military Intelligence contact had painted the unit with glowing-color brush strokes: "Koenig and his squadron are fearless, the archetype of the modern hero," he was told.

Koenig and his group!

When Mueller had earlier made Koenig's office his first stop, according to normal custom, the mighty Major looked up from behind his desk with a regal blandness he might have bestowed on a fly whose buzzing was causing him minor annoyance.

"Leutnant Fritz Mueller reporting for duty, sir!" said the just-noticed fly.

"Ah . . . yes," said the king. "Mueller. We've been expecting you." No return of the sharp salute, no rising in greeting, no command to stand at ease. Just the impression that, yes, the king had been informed of the servant's coming and now the servant appeared. Then: "Don't unpack yet, Leutnant."

"Sir?"

"I expect, Leutnant Mueller, you've brought your gear with you—other sets of freshly starched uniforms?"

"Yes, Herr Major. Outside . . ."

"Good. Don't unpack quite yet. I suggest you first meet some of the other people on base. I shall talk to you later. As you see, I am quite busy at the moment."

The Leutnant's eyes went from the Major's face to the top of his desk and back again. The only item on the clean desk was a cup of coffee.

"Yes, Herr Major."

"Dismissed, Leutnant."

Dismissed. Dismissed! No welcome, no happy to have you aboard, nothing. Simply dismissed. King.

And the group. Let us not forget the others. How could one forget the others? The dossiers that the young Australian had read were supposed to have been preparatory, but in fact, they did little to prepare him for that crew.

Example: Virginia (Ginny) Cabot; German alias, Elsa Dietrich. American. Boston blue blood. German language teacher, Vassar. Traveled extensively in Czechoslovakia during 30's. Friends from those days, mostly intellectuals, disappeared without trace after German invasion. Among them (name withheld), with whom MI presumes serious love affair. Germans believe her to be German Czech who favored their takeover. Twenty-nine years old. Expert in radio communications.

Ginny Cabot—rather, Elsa Dietrich—had an additional credential that the MI dossier failed to mention. Her tall willowy figure, her patrician face, and her long blonde hair all added up—in male mathematics—to a Viking vamp, provided one found favor with her, which the Australian appeared not to have done. He had met her at the base canteen, which she managed.

"Yes. Leutnant Mueller," she said coldly. "I have been informed you were coming. Do you expect you will be staying long?" She placed a cup of ersatz coffee before him on the canteen bar.

"Do I expect?" he repeated. When she didn't answer, he said, "What would *your* expectation be?"

She answered him without a trace of feeling. "I have little in the way of expectations, Herr Leutnant. I do my job, as best as I can, trusting that when Fate points its finger at me, it will be with some small spirit of benevolence."

"Look here, Miss Cabot . . ."

"Fräulein Dietrich! You have confused me with someone else."

He closed his eyes tightly, then opened them. The face he saw was deadly in its accusation. His voice lowered to a whisper. "I'm sorry."

"Death would make you sorrier, Herr Leutnant." Her eyes flashed. "A mistake like that, a mistaken identity statement like that, might—if the wrong ears were here to hear . . ."

"Yes, I know."

"You don't know, Leutnant Mueller. But know this —you've just failed your first test."

He had been half-sitting on the barstool before the counter. Now he was on his feet. "Failed? What test?"

"Sit down." There was no doubt about it. It was a command.

The Leutnant tried to change the mood by the full charm of his easy smile. But it didn't work, because the smile wasn't all that easy. Fortunately, Fate intervened, and Elsa's eyes left Mueller to focus somewhere behind him.

"Guten Morgen, Fräulein," came the lilting voice from over his shoulder.

The day's second example of the misleading nature of sketchy intelligence dossiers:

Alexander Lyle Plunkett; German alias, Oberleutnant Franz von Spiegel; twenty-eight years old. Fluent in German, Russian, Polish. Graduate of Edinburgh University. RAF liaison with Poles prior to German invasion, after which he narrowly escaped to Sweden. Aggressive and fearless pilot. Judo expert and skilled mountaineer.

That was the record. What the Australian saw in the flesh, however, was a slim blond man whose face looked almost feminine and whose manner of dress—a long silk scarf hanging over the front and back of one shoulder in some parody of a flying outfit—could best have been described as foppish. In point of fact, the Englishman struck Mueller as being the sissy brother-in-law of somebody important, a nobody allowed to play at the war game so that he'd be kept out of that important somebody's hair.

The Australian blinked his eyes to make absolutely certain that he was seeing clearly, and snapped to attention.

"Heil Hitler! Leutnant Fritz Mueller reporting for duty, Herr Oberleutnant von Spiegel!"

"It's Franz," came the reply. "Please, sit down."

"It's . . ."

"Franz. And I shall call you Fritz—unless you have some objection?"

"Ob—jection?" The Australian gulped, almost audibly. The high pitch of the other man's voice—the lisp—the immediate familiarity. Something felt suddenly creepy along the base of Leutnant Mueller's spine. . . .

"Er, no—I mean, yes. I have no objection." Mueller sat down again.

"That is good, Fritz," the slim man said with a suggestive wink. "I think it just may happen that we'll get along. Would you like that, Fritz—for the two of us to get along?"

The Australian's eyes shifted nervously away from

those of the other man. It was almost with a sense of pleading that they sought out the face of Elsa Dietrich. Her face, however, was blank—as if what she'd heard (if in fact she had heard) made no impression upon her one way or the other. Von Spiegel was speaking, but Mueller did not hear.

"Fritz? Is your mind wandering this morning?" The Oberleutnant's question was asked with an unexpected harshness.

"Franz? I'm not sure I know what you mean. I . . ."

"Your attention was wandering, young officer!"

"Perhaps it was, but I . . ."

"You have some idea, I suppose, of what might happen if two thousand feet over enemy territory you allow your attention to wander?"

The Australian's face flushed red. "Look here, Franz, I know perfectly well . . ."

"Herr Oberleutnant," said von Spiegel, rising slowly. "What?"

"You will address me by my rank. You will show that you have within yourself some awareness of military matters. You will recognize that you are a junior officer in the presence of a senior officer. You will *get off your backside and snap to attention! Now!*"

As Mueller saluted and clicked his heels, his face flushing hot and cold alternately, his ears picked up a sound something like a laugh, except that it was much too nasal —and it was coming from a spot too low, somewhere near the floor.

"Ah," the Oberleutnant said, with better humor. "The good Buergermeister himself has deigned to pay us a visit," he said, turning toward the door with a slight mock bow. "Come to inspect the young officer who wants to play pilot with us, have you, Buergermeister? Well, come along over then—come, come."

The Buergermeister obeyed the order by shuffling and scrambling across the wooden floor. Mueller looked out of the corner of his eye at the newcomer who had stopped at the Oberleutnant's side.

The Buergermeister was a short-haired black billy goat who looked well fed and cared for. Cocking his head at an odd angle, he let out with another prolonged, mocking laugh.

"Yes," the Oberleutnant said, turning to the woman behind the counter. "I've always said, Fräulein, that our dear Buergermeister Gruff is an excellent judge of people. Did you see how immediate his reaction was to our young visitor here?" The word *visitor* caused Mueller's mouth to open.

"Franz—might I suggest that enough is enough?"

Both men—and Buergermeister Gruff too—turned toward the speaker, a tall, broad, sandy-haired man whose open tunic collar showed the rank of Hauptmann. Not waiting for an answer to his question, the tall man smiled at the woman. "Fräulein Dietrich, I am in the mood for a little schnapps. Is that possible on this fine morning?"

"Possible, Hauptmann," she said lightly, "but not totally recommended."

"My doctor insists," he returned. Then, sitting down on one of the metal chairs, he leaned back and placed his left boot on the nearest tabletop. "Franz, join me if you like. You, too, Leutnant Mueller."

"I have things to attend to, Hauptmann Richter," von Spiegel replied. "Come, Buergermeister Gruff. No? Very well—stay and give the Hauptmann your best counsel in whatever he asks you."

The Hauptmann laughed when the Oberleutnant had gone, closing the door behind him. "It's all in knowing the right order to give. Come on over, Mueller—the lovely fräulein will give you a drink too, if you want one. Right, Elsa?"

Mueller sat down stiffly in the chair opposite the Hauptmann. He had no trouble recognizing this man from his dossier description! David Dean Smith; German alias Hauptmann Hans Richter. Thirty-two years old. Born in New York City, raised in Texas. Son of fairly well-off German immigrants, he spent boyhood summer vacations from school in Germany with an aunt. Air experience gained through barnstorming in U.S. and Europe. Hates Nazis because of unknown fate of aunt who opposed them openly and was sent to concentration camp. Possibly alive; Military Intelligence believes dead.

Hauptmann Richter spoke. "Mueller, you look—well —wary. As if I were going to bite you or something. Or is it something else?" His eyes narrowed. "You have something against Texans or what?"

Mueller's eyes almost popped. The last question had been asked in clear English—rather, in a clear Texan drawl.

The Australian cleared his throat. His English response came in a whisper: "Look, I've got no fight with Texans, or Yanks, or limeys for that matter. I'm here to fight Krauts, as you like to call them. Your enemy, I'm told, and hers." Mueller jabbed his thumb at Elsa, who was behind the counter drawing the Hauptmann's beer. "But she—and that odd one, the Englishman—they treat me as if *I* were the bloody enemy. What I don't understand is . . ."

"You forgot the Buergermeister," Richter interrupted.

"The bloody goat? What's he got to do with anything?"

"Evidently he doesn't much like you, either. I mean, why else would he suddenly have the urge to chew up your officer's cap?"

"*My cap!*" the young man cried aloud in English.

"Was," the Hauptmann corrected. "It now appears to be the Buergermeister's. Unless you have a use for the rather tattered portion that's left."

Elsa Dietrich laughed when Leutnant Mueller stamped out of the room and slammed the door behind him.

"A bit hard on him, weren't we?" Richter asked in German. He leaned against the counter and looked at the pretty woman who was drying glasses with a towel. She smiled and turned to put the glasses away on a high shelf. Richter admired her fine figure, and looked her up and down as she stretched to shelve the glassware. She saw him reflected in the long wall mirror and paused.

"As nice as your French dolls?" she said, staring at him in the mirror.

He flushed when he realized she had seen his rapt expression. She turned to face him and said, "I thought you'd have enough of eyeing women after spending every night in the past two weeks with that slutty barmaid. . . ."

Richter sighed and stood up. "For a Boston blue blood you sure do trouble yourself with the business of us country boys." He said it softly, and in English. "Maybe you oughta find some young French buck to calm you down, lady. I think you need either a lovin' or a spankin' to gentle you some."

She answered his challenge in her haughtiest Boston Brahmin manner. "Whatever it is I need, cowboy, you certainly won't be the one to administer it."

She stormed away into the back kitchen and left the door flapping emptily behind her. He hadn't intended his teasing to sound that biting. Somehow, no matter what he said to Elsa Dietrich, it seemed to come out wrong.

In the kitchen, Elsa listened to the outer door slam shut as Richter left. She poured herself a cup of ersatz coffee—a bitter drink of barley and chicory—and pushed back thoughts of Hans Richter/Dave Smith. From time to time, Ginny Cabot wondered what might have come of it all if she had met him as Dave Smith instead of as Hans Richter. Well, there was no point wondering about what could never be. They would have to put up with each other for as long as the Double Cross Squadron existed. And for as long as they managed to stay alive.

CHAPTER 5

Wednesday, 11 June

Once again Leutnant Mueller stood before the Herr Major Joachim Koenig. The MI material the Australian had been permitted to see had not been very specific about the man. In fact, all there was in the file was a sheet of paper with a badly focused photograph and six words. Joachim Koenig/John King: Staffel commander. The absence of any other detail had made the young man wonder if there was a criminal record in the Koenig's past.

"So, Mueller, I understand you've met several of my Staffel." The Major's German was clipped.

"I have met a few, yes, Herr Major."

"You met Fräulein Dietrich?"

"Yes, Herr Major."

"And you made a serious mistake."

"Yes, Herr Major."

"You met Oberleutnant von Spiegel?"

"Yes, Herr Major."

"And once again you erred."

"Sir?"

"You allowed him to anger you. There are many

German officers around like the Oberleutnant. Surely you must have met one or two by now."

"Yes, Herr Major. It is just that I did not expect . . ."

"You have aptly described the business we are in, Mueller. At any moment we can be faced with something we did not expect. We do not allow—cannot allow—ourselves to lose control. Even for an instant. You seem to have lost control over yourself and your emotions."

The young Australian swallowed hard. "Yes, Herr Major."

"And then you met our Hauptmann Richter. How did he impress you, Mueller?"

"He seemed friendly."

The Major spoke more slowly. "So he must have seemed, for it was with him that you committed your most serious error."

"I did what?"

"I believe you told him that you were here to fight—let me see, the word you used was *Krauts*. Furthermore, you told him so in English."

"But—but he . . ."

"He spoke English first. Is that what you were going to say?"

"Yes sir, but he also . . ."

"Was friendly, as you've already told me. He was understanding—and a real contrast to the Oberleutnant. They very often do that."

"The Hauptmann and the Oberleutnant?"

"No, Mueller. The Gestapo."

"The . . ." And then the young man saw the point. Mueller had heard of the technique before, a common police technique for grilling a suspect. The Hard Guy comes on first, and he treats you like dirt. Then comes the Soft Guy, Mr. Friendly Understanding. And you spill your guts out. He'd been set up and taken. Easily.

"You are right, Major," he said. "I lost the game."

"No. Game is not the right word, Mueller. You never had laid eyes on Hauptmann Richter before, and you opened up to him like he was a father confessor in a curtained box in some Melbourne parish. I want you to know something, Mueller. I told certain mutual acquaintances of ours that I wasn't sure I wanted you in the Double Cross Squadron."

Mueller nodded. "And now you've been proven right, is that it?" His eyes had been lowered, but now he raised them to meet the steady gaze of the man seated on the other side of the desk.

"Let me ask you a question, Mueller. Suppose you were flying one of our planes and you set down at an airstrip in Germany. You've seen the double crosses that our aircraft carry on the wings and fuselage?"

"Yes sir."

"Very well. Just after you step down from the plane, a Luftwaffe officer of higher rank approaches you. He remarks on the double crosses. He asks you why it is that your Staffel carries them. What is your answer—quickly!"

"Sir!" the Australian said, "Major Koenig's Staffel carries two crosses instead of one because of his objectives, objectives to which all of our unit members subscribe sincerely!"

"And . . . what objectives would that be, Leutnant?"

"To be twice as loyal to the Third Reich as the rest of the Luftwaffe. To render twice as much service, to fly twice as well, to sweat twice as much, to risk . . ."

"That is enough, Leutnant Mueller." Koenig seemed to be looking for something—something behind the eyes of the man who stood before him.

The Australian stared hard as well, but he kept his eyes an inch or two above those of his senior officer. The forehead scar was conveniently placed for that purpose.

There was a long pause before the Major spoke again. "Do you have any questions, Mueller, before you join your fellow pilots?"

The young man's eyes dropped and widened. "My *fellow* pilots . . ."

"You are a risk to the Double Cross Squadron, Mueller, but you are clever and intelligent. It is my hope that you are clever and intelligent enough to recognize those aspects of yourself that present a risk and then do something to control them. Check with Feldwebel Stumpf and he'll show you to your quarters. Any questions?"

"No, Herr Major."

"In that case, welcome aboard. By the way, somewhere along the line somebody must have told you that I'm a first-class bastard to work for—yes?"

"I have heard something like that, yes sir."

The scarred face softened. "Believe what you heard, Leutnant. In fact, believe that anything you heard was a gross understatement. Dismissed, Mueller."

With a click of his heels, Mueller turned toward the door. He had taken three steps when Koenig's voice stopped him.

"Hold up just a minute," the Major spoke sharply in English.

Heels clicked as the Leutnant about-faced smartly. "Herr Major?" he answered in German. "I failed to understand what I believe was spoken in the English language."

A smile spread on the squadron leader's face. "You may do after all, Mueller. You just may do."

"Thank you, Major, I shall try to show that you are correct. I shall . . ."

The door banged open and cut off whatever promise the new Staffel member was about to make. Wheeling around as if to defend himself from a rear attack, Mueller snapped to attention once more.

He recognized the SS uniform.

The SS officer spoke as if he were Hitler himself addressing another Munich gathering. "Herr Major Koenig, I have come because . . ."

"Moment," the Major said calmly as the telephone on his desk rang. "It might be urgent." He picked up the receiver. "Koenig."

"Gate watchman here, Herr Major," said the voice on the other end. "I wish to report that Sturmbannfuehrer von Stadt has passed through the gate and is presently on base. He expressed intention to visit the Herr Major and . . ."

"Excellent. I appreciate such advance early warning. Thank you."

"You are most wel—"

The receiver was down. "Nothing of any urgency," the Major said. "Well, von Stadt, welcome. You've come just in time to meet a new pilot in our Staffel. Leutnant Mueller, I present to you Sturmbannfuehrer Wolfgang von Stadt of our much praised Geheime Staatspolizei—Gestapo, for short."

"Gestapo? Nein! You know full well, Herr Major, that I am of the SS, not the Gestapo!"

"Ach!" Koenig said, as if he'd been corrected by an overly pedantic schoolmaster. "To be sure. But then both glorious branches of service report to our able and daring Reichsfuehrer Heinrich Himmler, do they not? Thus, I see little difference between them. Nonetheless, Leutnant Mueller, in our Sturmbannfuehrer here we are fortunate. We are most fortunate indeed to have such a man watching over us, believe me."

Mueller detected a suggestion of sarcasm in the Major's statement. For himself, he thought anybody in close proximity to the SS man before him was indeed unfortunate.

Von Stadt stood almost as tall as Hauptmann Richter, although there was nothing of the Hauptmann's strong build under the tightly tailored uniform of the SS Major. Von Stadt had the aura of a nasty bird of prey. His black, highly polished boots shifted nervously, as if ready to push off instantly from some lofty tree branch. The black-gloved hands played with each other, their long, tapered fingers suggestive of talons. Under the bald and polished crown of the man's head, dark lifeless eyes flicked about as if searching for an unwary victim, the scent of which had been detected by the sharp, beaked nose.

So deep was the impression the SS Major made upon Mueller that the younger man imagined he could smell the stench of death about the other.

"Well, Herr Major," von Stadt said, looking past Mueller as though he no longer existed. "I have some things to discuss with you. So if you have dismissed the Leutnant . . ."

"I have not dismissed him, Sturmbannfuehrer," Koenig interrupted. "In fact, I wish him to remain."

The lines in the face of the SS officer tightened. "Perhaps the Herr Major does not understand. I wish to discuss some matters that might be considered—ah, delicate."

"I assure the Sturmbannfuehrer that I understand perfectly. It is my wish to present to the Leutnant an example of how this Staffel cooperates with the Gestapo —er, the SS. He may have had misleading experiences that would suggest that those in the respective commands of my Reichsmarschall Goering and your Reichsfuehrer Himmler were sometimes antagonistic in their dealings with each other. It is my wish to dispel for this Leutnant any suggestion of such antagonism in this Staffel. Now—how might I be of assistance to you, my dear Sturmbannfuehrer?"

It was obvious to Mueller that the SS officer was not at all happy with Koenig's reply. It was clear von Stadt was unsure of the sincerity of Koenig's sentiment. His eyes flicked and fingers twitched uncomfortably.

"Very well then, Major. Last night, according to a full report I received this morning, one of your officers—von Spiegel, his name is."

"Oberleutnant Franz von Spiegel. Yes, Herr Sturmbannfuehrer?"

"Yes, well, last night he was in a café in the town, drinking heavily, according to the report."

"Ah, thank you for telling me, Sturmbannfuehrer. I shall speak to the Oberleutnant about it. Well, if that's all you've come to . . ."

"There's more!" the SS officer snapped. He was growing angry at the brusque treatment accorded him by Koenig. "He was most disorderly! There was—an altercation."

"Altercation," Koenig repeated.

"A fight, Herr Major. Two of my men were badly injured as a result."

"Two?" A right eyebrow cocked with the question. "Surely, two of your men, well trained as they are in unarmed combat . . ."

"It wasn't fair! This von Spiegel struck them from behind. A vicious and unwarranted attack that . . ."

The door to the office suddenly swung open. "Oh—I am so sorry," said Oberleutnant Franz von Spiegel. "I did not know you were occupied, Herr Major."

Mueller caught a quick exchange of glances between Koenig and von Spiegel. There was a veiled humor in the exchange, humor that the SS officer didn't see.

"Ah, Oberleutnant. We were just speaking of you. Please, close the door and come in. But first, was there anything of urgency that brought you here?"

"Nothing urgent, no sir. Just that there's a strange civilian in a trench coat walking around the base. I've never seen him before, and I wanted to be sure you knew of his presence. He seems to be inspecting things. My first impression was that he was some fool playing a private detective from one of those American films."

"No, Oberleutnant, I'm not aware of such a person." Koenig spoke to von Spiegel, but his eyes were on von Stadt.

The SS officer narrowed his eyes. "That would be my driver, Klemm. He is a new man. I asked him to wait outside by the car, but I assume he decided to have a look around. There is, I suppose, no harm in his doing so, Herr Major?"

Koenig shrugged. "Let him look all he wishes to." He turned to the Oberleutnant. "Our Sturmbannfuehrer tells me you had a bit of trouble last evening, Franz?"

"Trouble, sir?"

Von Stadt jabbed a finger at the Oberleutnant. "Look there, look at his hand! Let him try to deny he was fighting!"

"Oh, that," von Spiegel said matter-of-factly. "Yes, there was a bit of a scuffle."

Koenig nodded. "An altercation."

"One could call it that, yes sir."

"How did the altercation come about, Franz?"

"He was drinking!" the SS officer said accusingly.

"Drinking, yes, Herr Sturmbannfuehrer," the Oberleutnant agreed. "However, I think that was not so much a cause as was my knitting."

"Your *what?*" the Nazi sputtered.

"Knitting, sir. I'm making a sweater. Pink."

Mueller choked back the laugh that fought to erupt from his throat.

Koenig's voice took on a tone of mock sternness. "You were knitting, Franz. What happened then?"

"Well, sir, it is somewhat difficult to explain. I was minding my own business, knitting as I said, and these two SS officers appeared to find something humorous about what I was doing. They came over to my table to get a closer look—or so I thought. The next thing I knew, sir, they were saying things that, well, were rather embarrassing to me. Suggestive things about my manhood. I kindly requested them to leave me alone, but they were not disposed to do so. I endured their insults for as long as I could, sir, but then, well . . ."

"Continue, Franz," Koenig said.

"Well, when one of them reached over, pinched my cheek, and called me lovely sweetheart, I suppose I reacted."

"Reacted?" shrieked von Stadt. "Between them my two men have one broken jaw, six broken ribs, one broken wrist, a separated shoulder, one hip out of joint, and several smashed teeth. You call that reacting?"

The Oberleutnant looked at the tops of his boots. "Well, perhaps you might call it overreacting."

"You baited them, von Spiegel! You sat there in that café, knitting like some fairy princess—fully expecting someone to take the bait! I've had other reports of you doing things like this, but this is the first time any of my men were involved. Do you deny that you do this, that you have done this many times before?"

Von Spiegel looked innocently into the Sturmbann-fuehrer's cold eyes. "I cannot deny that on previous occasions I have been abused in drinking places and have had to defend myself; no, I cannot deny that, sir. I do deny, however, that there is anything wrong with knitting, wherever I choose to do it. I find knitting excellent for clearing the mind. It is also excellent for improving manual dexterity. If the Sturmbannfuehrer would wish, I would be happy to instruct him in the art. It is not difficult to learn, and it would not take much time for me to . . ."

"I do not want to learn knitting!"

"As the Sturmbannfuehrer wishes." Von Spiegel turned to his commander. "Is there anything else the Major requires of me?"

"No, Franz. You may go. Unless—Sturmbannfuehrer? Is any further clarification of the incident needed?" The smoldering face of the SS officer answered the question fully, but Koenig seemed not to see it. "Very well, then. That is all, Franz."

"Sir, about this Herr Klemm . . ."

"Klemm is an aide of our friend, the Sturmbannfueh-rer," Koenig interrupted. "He is to be offered every courtesy befitting that status."

"I understand, Herr Major," von Spiegel said. As he turned on his heel, his eye caught that of the Australian. He winked and strode in exaggerated military fashion to the door.

When von Spiegel was outside and the door closed behind him, Koenig sighed. "I apologize for this incident, Sturmbannfuehrer. The Oberleutnant has his eccentrici-ties, and they are somewhat trying at times. If the man were not such an excellent pilot . . . ah, well. But let's forget that. Was there something else you wished to discuss with me?"

The way Koenig asked the question told Mueller that he knew there was something else. For the moment, the SS officer was doing his best to swallow the bitterness of the von Spiegel affair. Von Stadt had not yet fully accomplished that distressing task when the silence following the Staffel commander's question caused him to fill the uncomfortable vacuum.

"Yes. There was an attack on one of our installations last night, Major. A warehouse. Evidently it was the maquis."

"I heard about it. One of your men mentioned it to me last night."

The SS officer licked his lips. "Yes. In any case, the damage done was not all that severe, and we'll have our revenge soon enough. Soon enough." Von Stadt's cruel eyes glinted as he went on, "We've rounded up a few Frenchmen already. Those scum will be sorry they were ever born, and even more sorry they dared defy the Reich! This shall stop!" The officer's voice rose. "This shall not go on! No! This insolence shall not go unpunished! I'll uphold the honor of the Reich! I swear—"

"Von Stadt!" Koenig cut in sharply. "I presume, Herr Sturmbannfuehrer, that you did not come out to our Staffel to tell me about some petty sabotage."

"Ach, yes," said von Stadt, and his beady eyes began to search Koenig as he spoke. "Of course, Herr Major. My visit today regards a report which was given to me by one of my men. The report concerns you and a certain—"

"You have a report on *me*, Sturmbannfuehrer?" Koenig's voice suddenly was unfriendly.

"It is but routine, Major, only routine. However, the officer who made out the report says that you refused to divulge what you were doing out on the roadway at that time of night—or morning, I should say."

"His report is correct."

"Is . . . correct. Well, yes, but . . . you see, Major, the way we work—well, surely you see the need to—"

"To pry into my private affairs?"

"You yourself, Major, first told the officer something about sharing someone's bed."

"And you wish to know whose bed. I find it difficult to believe you are that much of a busybody, Sturmbannfuehrer."

Von Stadt stiffened. "You know very well, Major, that

much information can be gained from—er, that is, from sexual tactics."

"Any sexual tactics I perform, Herr Sturmbannfuehrer, do not have as their objective the giving or receiving of information, military or otherwise. You may be assured of that."

"The road you were on, Major. It leads back to a lightly populated area. In fact it would be a simple matter for my men to visit the few houses out that way and question the inhabitants. I have the idea you might not like that."

"You are right. Such an action—taking place at a particular house—might strain the up-to-now excellent relationship you and I have established between ourselves. That would not be productive for the Reich."

"Nonetheless, Herr Major. The SS did not gain its reputation for thoroughness without cause. If you refuse to answer, I am afraid I must carry out such an investigation."

"Very well, Sturmbannfuehrer. I will cooperate with you, but only if I have your word as an officer that no written record will be made of what I tell you."

"You have it," the SS officer said. Mueller could see von Stadt already alerting his mind to recall word-for-word the Staffel commander's statement, to be jotted down immediately upon leaving the office. Koenig began:

"The Countess von Coburg . . ."

"Is crippled! Surely you are not asking me to believe—"

"Are you a man of such little imagination, Sturmbannfuehrer?"

"But—but, I mean how . . . I mean, if I were you and had, right here on my own base, a woman such as the lovely Fräulein Dietrich . . ."

"You find the fräulein attractive, Sturmbannfuehrer?"

"She—she is at least not crippled from the waist down, as is this Countess who cannot . . ."

"You emphasize the *cannot*, Herr Sturmbannfuehrer," Koenig said quietly. "I am thinking mainly of the *can*—the *can* that makes anything possible for one with wealth. And the Countess, as you know, has great wealth."

There was a pause as the SS officer considered this. Koenig interrupted:

"The war will not last forever. When the end comes and our hands no longer carry weapons, I wish my own hands to hold a good bit of the von Coburg wealth. Now, if you, or any of your men, do anything—anything—to adversely affect this delicate venture of mine . . ."

"Surely not!" von Stadt blurted out. He was smiling —it was more of a lecherous sneer. To von Stadt, there was now a sense of kindred souls communicating. "Surely, surely not, Herr Major. I shall issue such instructions immediately upon returning to my office. I shall place the von Coburg estate totally out of bounds to my subordinates."

"I am deeply in your debt, Herr Sturmbannfuehrer," Koenig said. "I must think how I can repay you."

"There is one way. England. I have heard that you visit a certain secret place there."

Mueller saw Koenig suddenly freeze. "What is it you have heard?" the Major asked slowly, warily.

"A rumor only, of course. From Berlin. Reichsmarschall Goering is said to have spoken of it to—to some of his high-level colleagues. He said his personal and special Double Cross Staffel has access to a secret base in England, which is a trading market for information and . . . for other things."

"An interesting rumor," Koenig said, the tension now completely gone. "If there were some truth in it."

"Yes, well, if—if there were such a place, I would like —I mean, if it could be arranged for me to visit, I would be very grateful."

"I understand, Sturmbannfuehrer. Perhaps . . ."

"Yes?"

"Perhaps I shall investigate whether or not this place exists for SS officers."

"Yes, Herr Major, I would appreciate your doing that." The SS Sturmbannfuehrer and the Luftwaffe Major smiled at one another. It was a moment of shared understanding.

But only a moment. It ended abruptly as the door

crashed open. The short, ox-faced man standing there looked like he had traveled on his stomach through a particularly messy part of hell. His face and hair and what was once a neatly pressed trench coat were covered with dark, wet mud. The impression the man made was as striking to the nose as to the eye.

"Klemm!" the Sturmbannfuehrer was aghast.

"Inspecting the area behind the kitchen, I see," Koenig said without emotion. "Pigs used to be kept there when this place was a farm. Still haven't been able to do much about cleaning it up, I'm afraid."

"Idiot!" stormed von Stadt. "How did this happen?"

"One of the Staffel's officers, sir," the stinking man began. "Kind of strange—girlish in a way, if you know what I mean . . ."

The Sturmbannfuehrer's eyes snapped to Koenig's and then back to his own man. "He attacked you?"

"Oh no, sir, not at all! He was helping me, showing me around, in fact. He said he'd been told to show me every courtesy."

"Well, then, what happened?"

"We were around behind the kitchens, as the Herr Major said, and the Oberleutnant saw something on the ground—just at the edge of this old pigsty. It was a five mark piece, shining in the sun. Well, of course, I bent down to pick it up—and the next thing I knew . . ." Klemm looked sourly at his clothes.

"Well what, idiot?"

"This animal, sir! From out of nowhere, this *goat* . . ."

CHAPTER 6

Wednesday, 11 June

There were four things in his large plush Berlin office in which Reichsmarschall Hermann Goering took special pride this afternoon. Three of them he had taken pleasure in for some time: the ornate desk that once had belonged to a fifteenth century Italian by the name of Borgia; the Reich flag, a huge red, white and black swastika which dominated one complete wall of the office; and the outsized oil painting of the Fuehrer, the painting which Goering himself had commissioned and which looked down from its place on the wall behind the Reichsmarschall's chair with special favor on the man who sat there.

The fourth item that delighted Goering was the new bone-white uniform he sported. The latest in the line of personally designed outfits, this particular one, in the Reichsmarschall's opinion, was especially well-executed. He was especially pleased with the look of the third and newest line of gold piping around the collar and shoulder boards. He had been concerned that the addition might look a bit too garish when actually completed, but this morning his mirrored image satisfied him fully.

There was, however, in the office this afternoon something that did not please the Reichsmarschall. That something was a man who sat on the opposite side of the desk quietly polishing the glass of his silver pince-nez. Reichsfuehrer Heinrich Himmler had been seated there for some ten minutes now, the stated reason for his visit being an exchange of views about the impending Nazi push eastward. The exchange was, as usual between these two, less than frank. It could not be otherwise given the intense rivalry between them. The Reichsmarschall fenced gracefully with Himmler's false pleasantries and banalities until such time as the former chicken farmer got around to the real business that had brought him to Goering's office. It was when Himmler placed his pince-nez back into position on his nose that his tone of voice altered, alerting Goering that the Reichsfuehrer's real business was at hand.

"I suppose the Reichsmarschall will be committing much of his air forces to the attack on Russia."

"You suppose correctly, yes."

"Tell me, Reichsmarschall—would that include your prized Double Cross Squadron, the one you have based at Lisieux?"

Goering hesitated before answering. When he did, it was with a question: "Why is that small group of any interest to you, Reichsfuehrer?"

A slight shrug. "It's not really of interest—not in and of itself. It is just that I have been hearing much of it lately."

"Through your own channels?"

"Yes. I have a man stationed near there. Von Stadt. Not among my service's best, but one who very often reports things to me directly, out of channels."

Goering smiled. "I've heard something of the man. Perhaps his directness with you has something to do with the manner in which he received his appointment. I understand he is the brother-in-law of a very lovely woman whose accomplishments in your bed chamber are much appreciated."

"That is a rumor without foundation!"

Goering's smile broadened. "I am happy to hear you say so, Reichsfuehrer. I for one have never credited the story much. Surely the opportunity to give pleasure to such an overworked leader as yourself would be considered by any loyal woman of the Reich as its own reward."

"I have not come here to discuss women!"

"Ah, then what have you come for, Heinrich?"

"We were discussing your Double Cross Squadron. You still haven't told me whether you were intending to deploy it in the push to the east." Himmler said.

"It is not a combat squadron, Heinrich. It does mainly reconnaissance work and—other service."

"Yes, personal service—for the Reichsmarschall."

"For the Reich, Heinrich. They serve the Reich."

As soon as the words left his mouth, the Reichsmarschall had the uncomfortable feeling that he was falling into a trap.

"That is good to hear, Hermann, very good to hear. For, you see, if your Staffel does not have to be occupied in the preparation for the Fuehrer's glorious move east, it can be of very special service to the Reich in another matter—and to the Fuehrer, with whom I have already discussed the matter."

"You have discussed my Double Cross Staffel with the Fuehrer?"

Himmler obviously was enjoying the Luftwaffe leader's discomfort. "No, of course not. The suspicions expressed by von Stadt are without any substance, just a feeling on his part. No, Hermann, what I have discussed with the Fuehrer is the need to better penetrate British Intelligence. Of course, our successes to date have been commendable, mind you."

"I'll not argue that point," Goering said in a way that left little doubt that he believed the point could be argued, if he chose to do so.

"Yes, well, in any event, the Fuehrer has agreed with my plan to put a very special agent into England. You may have heard of an agent, Falke, who also is referred to as the Falcon? A very accomplished worker for the Reich."

"I may have, I don't recall. But I fail to see how this concerns my squadron at Lisieux."

"It concerns them directly, Reichsmarschall. You have on occasion mentioned the existence of a secret air base in England where—where a black market operates. A base to which your Double Cross Staffel appears to have special access."

"Go on."

"Well, it has occurred to me that this base would be a perfect drop-off for my agent Falke. Since your people know where it is and have had such success getting into the place and out of it again unscathed, it naturally occurred to me that you and I might cooperate on this operation—one of your birds taking my falcon. It also occurred to me that such cooperation between us, when it became known to others, might be good in itself. You know, Reichsmarschall, there are some in high command who believe the two of us are on something other than the best of terms. Such a joint operation would serve to dispel such—ah —misguided beliefs."

Yes, thought Goering, and it also might give Herr Himmler the opportunity to get one of his top agents in a position to pry into the operation of the Lisieux Staffel. Not to mention discovering the closely guarded location of the English base that had provided Goering, through Koenig, with bits of information that the Fuehrer himself found extremely interesting—sometimes interesting enough to wonder quite loudly why it was that the Luftwaffe so often seemed to have more valuable intelligence than Himmler's secret services, which were charged with that responsibility.

"Do you agree to cooperate with my plan, Reichsmarschall? I really don't see how you can object."

Goering considered Himmler's still-smiling face. He didn't like the face or the idea. There were other ways to get agents into Britain, other ways that had proven workable. Why did Himmler now decide on this way? What was his real game? To latch onto some bit of information that would be incriminating to the Staffel and therefore undermine Goering himself? The loyalty of Koenig and his hand-picked men was not to be questioned, of that Goering was certain. But he had seen Himmler's people at work. One little fact—one little innocent fact, twisted just so —could effectively raise a doubt, which in turn could bring disaster down upon the head of the unwary victim.

"Hermann?" Himmler said softly.

"When do we begin this plan? What do you see as the right moment?"

"A matter of days, Hermann—a week at most. This, I assume, will suffice to give your people enough—ah, warning? Yes?"

The Reichsmarschall forced a smile to his lips to match that of the other man. "I suppose it will have to, Heinrich. It will have to suffice, won't it?"

Chapter 7

At 1:20 p.m., the Countess von Coburg wheeled her chair over to the silver tea tray the white-haired butler had left on the low oak table in the drawing room. With elegant style she poured tea into two bone china cups and extended one to the German officer who sat comfortably on the couch.

"They are being very cautious about this," she said.

"They have reason to be," Major Joachim Koenig replied. "They must know that industrial diamonds are in short supply on both sides these days. At the moment, the key question is when will they ship them?"

"That is no longer the key question. Monday night is your answer."

Koenig considered. "That hardly leaves us much time."

"I also am not certain whether the knowledge we have can be put to any practical use by you or anyone else."

"That is something for us to talk about."

She smiled suggestively. "As usual, you are so certain of yourself."

"Is there any loyal officer of the Third Reich who is not certain of himself?"

She shook her head. "I suppose not. In that respect, at least, you are very convincing. How does the ring feel?"

Koenig spread the fingers of his left hand and looked down at the antique gold ring that he'd placed on his little finger a few minutes before. The large oval face of the seal ring was composed of a lion and a hawk holding up a shield divided into four sections which in turn contained a bow and arrow, a quill pen, a five-pointed star, and an Egyptian pyramid.

"Whoever had the von Coburg crest designed obviously fancied the family to be of excellence in just about everything."

"Designers of crests always do. I asked you how it felt."

"Heavy. An encumbrance to proper hand movement. But nonetheless necessary to convince von Stadt that I am pursuing you successfully."

"I understand," she said. "Von Stadt shall see you're something special to the Countess von Coburg."

"And, more meaningfully, she is important to me."

"You mean you're not just trying to get your hands on the late count's wealth?"

He nodded. "That too—the ring is to remind me and von Stadt that I'm really trying to cash in on the late count's widow. In the deepest recesses of his wormlike heart, von Stadt knows that I'd like nothing better than to snap his neck. I've now elevated you to become the straw that, if ever touched by him, would cause me to take such delightful action."

"And you're certain that will give him cause to keep away from this estate?"

"I am. But, Madame Countess, let us forget von Stadt for the moment and go on to the main subject."

She smiled. "The details of what we've learned are in the envelope you'll receive before leaving. There is a map route shown there. It is the route the vehicle carrying the diamonds will take to the armament factories on the coast —unless something intervenes."

"Something or someone."

"Which brings us back to von Stadt."

"Continue."

"When you have reviewed the material in the envelope, you will know that von Stadt is the key to the operation in several ways. First, the actual route the diamonds will go—and the diversions—have been devised by him. This man is not a fool, whatever you choose to think. Second, and more important, the diamonds will be controlled in their movements by orders which are preceded by a secret code word."

"We know that, but we don't know the code word."

"That is something that is known only by von Stadt and his superiors."

"Somebody has a lot of faith in our Sturmbannfuehrer."

"Faith in the SS. Now you can gain some appreciation for just how important this shipment of diamonds is to the Nazis. Security will be tight, very tight. So tight, in fact, that I don't see how—"

"I want those diamonds," he said levelly.

"Then it just may be that you will have to get them yourself." Her words were brusque, but she shook her head slightly. "Look, John—I would like to help, but what you're asking would amount to a full military confrontation. We in the maquis are capable of disruption, of taking out bridges and warehouses and an occasional lightly guarded patrol. But we are not an army, we are not a powerful armed force that can simply march up and overpower the SS."

Her face hardened and her eyes became distant as she said, "If we could, we would stop them from taking our villagers prisoner, torturing them, killing them. . . ." She looked up at Koenig, and he saw sorrow deep within her eyes. "That swine von Stadt—"

The Countess let her gaze drop to the floor. She sighed

once, then looked back at Koenig. "We cannot, however, overpower the SS."

"We need brains. Not force. We must take the diamonds by stealth. That's what the maquis is good at doing."

"We'll discuss this another time."

"Damn it, today is Thursday—we've got only four more days."

"I said we'll discuss this another time, and that is the way it will be! I'm not one of your junior officers, nor am I just another woman who finds your charms so irresistible that she can't wait until you hop into her bed!"

"No, Simone," he said quietly. "Not just another woman who finds me irresistible. For me, you're *the* woman who can't resist me."

That made her smile. When she saw his answering smile, she couldn't restrain a laugh. Then, suddenly, the laugh died, the smile was gone.

"John, please don't die. Please."

He looked into her eyes, then turned away. "If I do, dear Countess, at least I shall be wearing your ring."

He'd meant it to sound lighthearted, but it somehow didn't come out that way. In silence they drank their tea.

"Von Stadt wants *what*?"

Upon returning to base, Koenig had called a meeting in his office for his three pilots. He had barely begun introducing the purpose of the special gathering when Hauptmann Richter had interrupted.

"While you were away this afternoon, you received a telephone call from our favorite Sturmbannfuehrer. I took it in your absence."

"What did the gentleman have to say?"

Richter told him.

"He wants *what*?"

"Just a simple secret chauffeuring service, which is, of course, one of our prime missions as a unit, yes? But it's not just von Stadt who wants it. Himmler, and Goering too, if our friend is to be believed."

With which Richter handed his superior officer a

teletype. The message, for the attention of Joachim Koenig, read:

REICHSFUEHRER HIMMLER HAS REQUESTED, AND I
HAVE GIVEN ASSENT, THAT THE SERVICES OF YOUR
STAFFEL BE EMPLOYED IN A MISSION CONCERNING
AN SS AGENT KNOWN BY NAME FALKE. I PERSONALLY
REQUEST YOUR FULLEST COOPERATION IN THIS
MATTER. DETAILS TO BE COMMUNICATED TO YOU BY
HIMMLER'S LOCAL MAN. GOERING.

"Let's have the details, Hauptmann." Koenig said.

"Details, Herr Major!" Hauptmann Richter snapped. "At about 1 p.m., Monday, 16 June, an aircraft of this Staffel will land at our glorious Luftwaffe base at Nantes. Shortly thereafter, said aircraft will depart said Nantes base with SS agent Falke aboard."

"Destination?"

"Here."

"Here?"

"Only a preliminary destination, Major. A stopover. As soon as possible, we are to remove said agent Falke to Merry England via the MI air base there. The agent will blend into the landscape and no doubt perform for the glory of the Third Reich, not to mention for the glory of Heinrich Himmler."

"When do we take Falke to England?"

The Hauptmann shrugged. "That appears to be up to us, Major. Von Stadt hopes it wouldn't take more than a week or so, however."

Koenig's eyes narrowed. "It won't take more than twenty-four hours. We can't afford Himmler's spies probing around this base for an extended period."

"This agent," Richter said, "has us as his assignment?"

Koenig shook his head. "It's not likely that we are his primary assignment, no. But Himmler would like nothing better than to find something—no matter how slight—with which to embarrass Goering. I want this Falke in and out of here so fast his memory of the place will be a fuzzy blur."

"How about arranging for no memory at all?" It was the musical voice of Oberleutnant von Spiegel. "Why should he ever arrive in the first place? Why should there not be —say, a mechanical failure of the aircraft? One that would cause an evacuation of the plane. One in which our pilot —naturally familiar with emergency evacuation procedures —parachutes safely to the ground, but all too unfortunately this Falke person, not familiar with emergency—"

"No," Koenig interrupted. "No, for several reasons, one of them being that we have a reputation to live up to. Furthermore, if this agent is lost in the manner you suggest, all we will have accomplished is the appointment of another agent—perhaps one with us as his subject. Himmler's set on getting one of his special people into Britain. The longer we can make him think he's been successful at that, the better off our teammates across the Channel—and we—will be."

"So we bring Falke here. And then to England."

"Correct, Hauptmann. We do exactly that, and we deliver Falke on a silver platter to our Uncle Freddy."

"End of Falke," von Spiegel said. "Same idea as mine, actually."

"Not quite," Hauptmann Richter said. "The Major's way, our military intelligence gets to talk to Falke."

Koenig, his brow furrowed in thought, nodded slowly to himself. "All right. The timing is bad because we'll be busy getting the diamonds, but we don't seem to have a choice—we must play host to Himmler's falcon. First, however, we play host to the Reichsfuehrer's vulture—von Stadt. Hauptmann, it would be appropriate if Fräulein Dietrich were to radio our kind Uncle Freddy that he should make preparations for a party of three fun-seekers to officially inaugurate his establishment this Sunday."

"This Sunday?" Richter repeated. "That's not much time."

"The message, which I entrust you to compose, should make clear that the visit will include von Stadt, and its success is vital if our kind uncle wishes certain family jewels to change families."

Koenig extended a manila envelope to von Spiegel. "Oberleutnant, what currently is known about the movement of the diamonds is all in here. Give the matter your fullest attention. I will expect your recommended method of intercepting them by this time tomorrow. In working out your plan, assume that we can at best expect only diversionary support from the maquis. Also assume that we will have only three operatives—you, Hauptmann Richter, and myself."

"If it pleases the Major," Leutnant Mueller spoke up, "I am familiar with ground operations."

"Leutnant, you will be occupied with other matters. Namely, Herr Himmler's falcon."

A look of doubt crossed Leutnant Mueller's face, but it was there for only an instant. "Anything else I should assume, Major?" asked von Spiegel.

"Yes." He paused. "Assume we know the code word which will enable us to reroute the diamonds as we choose. Also, if practical, design the action so that after we get the diamonds, we will have the maximum amount of time before the Nazis discover what has taken place."

Von Spiegel smiled. "A truly intellectual challenge, Herr Major, but one that I am delighted to accept. One point, however, I should think we require a strategy to fall back on, in the event this code word is not discovered."

"Von Stadt possesses that word. We will have him share it with us."

Richter's eyes flashed. "Ah! Our message to our kind uncle will underline the importance of our Sunday outing. But I wonder, Major, if the strategy will ensure learning the code word."

Koenig nodded. "As the Oberleutnant has said, a fall-back strategy is necessary. One should be devised for Monday night; I have another in mind for Sunday night—if our afternoon with Percy Bellows fails us."

Von Spiegel's grin broadened. "If the Major is considering beating the information out of our Sturmbannfuehrer, and if he is calling for volunteers—"

Richter interrupted. "Sorry, Oberleutnant. I outrank you and therefore claim that privilege for myself."

"I'm not seeking that kind of volunteer," Koenig said. "No, not this time. This time . . ." His tone suddenly had become grim, then it changed back to its usual matter-of-factness. "All right, that's it for now. Hauptmann, please tell Fräulein Dietrich that after she has communicated with Uncle Freddy, I would appreciate having a word with her."

"Sir?" Richter's eyebrows were knitted. "I—I would appreciate having a word with the Herr Major. In private. Now."

Koenig nodded. "Very well, Hauptmann. If you other gentlemen will excuse us?"

When the two were alone, the silence in the office was thick with tension, most of it coming from Richter's side of the desk.

"Let's have it," the Major said.

"I think I know what the Herr Major has in mind for Fräulein Dietrich."

"Our Sturmbannfuehrer finds Elsa Dietrich very attractive," Koenig said.

"But you can't ask her to—"

"I can and will, if it proves necessary. She happens to be part of this war, too. She happens to be part of our team, and she happens to possess weapons that the rest of us lack."

"I don't like the idea of her using them with von Stadt. The thought of it almost makes me puke."

"I don't like the idea either. It may not be necessary, but if so, then it shall be done."

Richter's fists were clenched tightly. "If it is, Herr Major—if it is—and if the day ever comes when a volunteer is needed to plaster that slimy—"

"I will not seek volunteers, Herr Hauptmann," Koenig said quietly. "The assignment will be yours."

CHAPTER 8

Sunday, 15 June

At midday the sky over the English Channel was leaden. The good weather of the first half of the month suddenly had been washed away in murky drizzle. It was not an optimal day for flying, as von Stadt's stomach repeatedly communicated to him.

The paper bag! He gagged, his bugged-out eyes searching frantically around the confined space to which he'd been assigned on the floor of the Me 110's cockpit, between Koenig in front and Richter behind. Finding the bag between his pressed-together knees, he opened it with twitching fingers, the black-gloved coverings of which already bore small spattered reminders of the two previous occasions upon which the paper container had been used.

In the rear seat of the Messerschmitt 110, Hauptmann Richter closed his eyes, wishing he could also close his nose to von Stadt's awful misery. The Nazi was in the space between himself and the pilot in the front of the dipping, veering aircraft. The twin-engined 110 featured a roomy cockpit—for two—which seemed much less roomy when, as now, a third person and freight boxes were added.

"Herr Major," Richter said over the intercom, his tightly clenched jaws adding a rasping sound to the normal crackle of the headset. "I trust that most of the tossing about is because of the weather."

"What do you think, Herr Hauptmann?" came Koenig's reply.

"Might I request a small measure of mercy?"

"For our beloved Sturmbannfuehrer or for yourself, Hauptmann?"

Richter opened his left eye and looked in the direction of the SS officer who, lacking a headset, could not overhear the conversation over the roar of the engine. At the moment, his contribution would not have been appreciated. Richter winced. "God in heaven . . ."

"Excellent, Hauptmann. You have demonstrated once more the effectiveness of the power of prayer."

And it was as if someone suddenly had withdrawn the curtain of gray to reveal powerful floodlights trained on the brilliant landscape below. Richter recognized their position immediately from the white cliffs and, beyond them, the listening stations with antiaircraft gun emplacements dotting the green and brown checkerboard.

"Over England!" he called to von Stadt. The SS officer's face was slightly green-tinted, and he could manage only a weak, short-lived twitch of the lips that might have been the beginning of a smile of relief.

Sitting up as straight as he could, von Stadt peered out of the cockpit. "So . . . this is England. . . ."

"Major," Richter said into his headset. "I hate to mention it, but our passenger is having himself a good look at our route."

"Thank you, Hauptmann. You may wish to explain to him the purpose of our next maneuver."

With that, the 110 suddenly was thrown into a roll and began a steep climb that lasted a full ten seconds. At the top of the climb, the plane spun over again and flipped, nosedown, into a shuddering dive.

"Diversionary tactics!" Richter shouted.

"*Uurrgghh—ahh!*" von Stadt acknowledged, retching.

"Oh, God! . . ." Richter suffered.

Koenig's voice crackled. "More prayer, Hauptmann?"

"Was that a laugh I just heard, Herr Major?"

"I was led to believe you appreciated a sense of humor, Hauptmann."

Richter's nostrils quivered in rebellion. "If things get any more humorous, Major, I'm going to have to step out for a breath of fresh air."

"I can't believe . . . we are in . . . England!" Von Stadt's face still had its pale green cast and he moved unsteadily from the plane. "This—this is . . ." He didn't have the words to complete the thought, whatever it might have been.

Koenig was his usual stoneface, but Richter could not help the grin that took over his own features. A good part of the reason for his high spirits was the smell of clean air; a second cause was the obvious and admirable way dear Uncle Freddy Standish had prepared for their visit. Richter could well understand the SS officer's amazement, for the Hauptmann was not a little amazed himself. In the short time of warning that had been given, Standish had outdone himself.

Even from the air, the place hardly resembled the peaceful airstrip he had visited just five days ago. The field was heavily guarded with sentry boxes and barbed wire which had not been present before. But the ground view was even more spectacular. Where before there had been only a dozen aircraft in a neat formation, the field now contained almost three times that number. Where formerly there had been a few men efficiently working—men without insignia, seemingly without speech—there now were some twenty men relaxing around the aircraft and the four hangar buildings. Wearing a variety of uniform colors and patterns, all were chatting good-naturedly. Most held mugs or glasses which contained potent beverages.

"Mein Gott! Who—"

"Visitors, Sturmbannfuehrer," Koenig said. "Just like us."

"But the uniforms! The airplanes—their markings!"

As Richter took a closer look, he was even more impressed with the panorama of foreign craft that intermingled with the British Spitfires and Hurricanes. Those he recognized included an American Bell Aircobra fighter complete with a shark's mouth painted on the nose; an Italian Fiat Falco biplane that looked like it had been hastily imported from a Renaissance museum; a Russian four-seater Ilyushin bomber and—Lord Almighty—a Jap Aichi fighter. Where in hell that thing came from was anybody's guess. In fact, one might accuse Standish of overdoing things a mite with that one.

"There are German planes here, too," the SS officer said, still in a state of shock.

"There are," Koenig confirmed. Turning directly to face the Sturmbannfuehrer, he spoke with a heavy menace. "Listen to me carefully, von Stadt. You are here as a guest —my personal guest. If you have any questions about what you see here, you will ask only me or Hauptmann Richter —no one else. The rules here are few, but one of the primary rules is that everybody minds his own business. There is no war here, von Stadt. There is only business and pleasure and a certain kind of comradeship that develops only among a select group of elite men who are skilled at what they do. Tomorrow one of these pilots may be sending to a flaming death the very man with whom he's drinking and laughing right now. Each of them knows that possibility exists. Each of them forgets that bit of reality now. In more precise terms, Sturmbannfuehrer, this place is not a reality. It is a respite from the real world of bullets and bombs, and these men and we are privileged to be here. Do you understand me?"

"I shall say nothing to anyone here."

"You need not go that far, Sturmbannfuehrer. Just be careful what you say. There have been two or three occasions, I'm told, when first-time guests were not prudent." Koenig paused ominously. "They never left this place alive. This air base has its own laws, von Stadt, and it is permitted by the British to exist on their soil because it is of value to their agents, who make use of it. But other agents come here, and they too profit from their visits, as you shall soon see."

After another pause in which Koenig saw his message sink in, he turned to Richter. "Now—where to begin? Might I suggest that our guest try his hand at the gaming tables? You've brought money, I trust, von Stadt."

"Some, yes."

"Good. Hauptmann, kindly accompany our guest to the exchange facilities. It might afford a good opportunity for him to meet personally with Mr. Bellows—if, that is, Percy can spare the time."

Richter nodded. "Percy usually can spare a moment for first-time guests. He likes to spot those who might turn out to be troublemakers early in the game. Come with me, Sturmbannfuehrer."

"Bellows—Percy?"

"He runs things around here," Richter explained. "A fair man, in his way, I suppose. Except . . . well, if he should happen to take a dislike to someone . . . But I shouldn't worry about that if I were you, Sturmbannfuehrer. Percy will like you. Shall we go?"

The cheerful sounds from the gaming tables and the bar on the other side of the office door did not contribute to clear thinking. But in just five minutes of conversation, Koenig and Colonel Standish had worked out a plan of action. The skeletal British colonel used the telephone to brief a third man on the plan. When the phone was back in its cradle, Standish pursed his lips, as if in doubt.

"You really think this will work, John?"

"Percy is good, Freddy. Von Stadt is greedy."

"Both perhaps true—the first statement definitely, the second probably. But your von Stadt would appear, from what you've told me, to be full of false bravado."

"That's why I suggested using Percy. He's very good at frightening people."

Standish looked at the Luftwaffe pilot steadily. "So is Himmler, I understand. Well, we can't lose anything by trying this, can we? And we believe the stakes are worth the effort—as you can see from our other preparations here."

"For which, congratulations. You must have pulled in every unemployed actor in Britain for the job."

Standish smiled. "Most were already employed—by Military Intelligence. I like to keep as much of this as possible within the family."

"Speaking of family, I've got a bit of a problem with a member of the other side's family. Have you heard of a German agent who goes by the name Falke?"

"Falcon? Suggestive name, but no, I can't recall anything. Should I have heard anything?"

"I would do some checking if I were you. Before the day after tomorrow."

"That's when you bring the diamonds—I hope."

"That's when I also will bring you this Falke."

"Here? You plan to bring a German agent here? Why?"

Koenig smiled. "To end the falcon's last flight."

"Fourteen, even, low, red." The croupier's voice was as flat as the table. The voice of Sturmbannfuehrer von Stadt, however, was jubilant.

"Richter! I have won again—on red and even! How many marks worth of chips have I now?"

"Four hundred and fifty something, Sturmbannfuehrer. You are doing very well, very well indeed."

"I love this place, Richter—it is fantastic, simply fantastic!" As the SS officer leaned out to place his chips again on even, red, the twelve numbers in the center vertical row, Hauptmann Richter grinned. A few hours before, von Stadt had not been in such harmony with what he'd found.

Percy Bellows had not been available when they'd gone to pay a courtesy call at his office. While waiting, they went to the rows of tables set end-to-end—two dozen trading stalls that filled the building. Richter suggested they tour them first. He was not surprised at von Stadt's reaction as they passed the first booth.

"Hauptmann—those are German machine pistols!"

"Correct. You will also find weapons used by the British, the Russians, the Finns—just about everybody. Weapons-trade is brisk, but harmless. Most of it is of the souvenir variety. Fliers can't easily get to the aftermath of ground battles to collect for themselves."

"But those—they are new! They look as though they have come here direct from our factories."

"Probably they did. I trust the trader got what he wanted for them, either in cash or barter. Most everyone doing business here does so to his complete satisfaction. The man trading those guns, for example, might well have received—well, for example, look in this stall over here, Sturmbannfuehrer."

The SS officer could not believe his eyes as Richter led him past stall after stall which offered goods for sale or suitable trade. The goods ranged from precision chronometers to military arms and other equipment, such as aerial cameras and manuals for assembling and repairing them, to more mundane items which were scarce in these times: spark plugs, batteries, ball bearings, and a host of various machine parts. Luxury items were also in abundance—fine china, silver flatware, and, to bless such tableware, good Russian caviar.

On the side of the great hall opposite the stall where von Stadt had seen the German machine pistols, Richter led the way to a stall that dealt in adult magazines and books. It was tended by a toothless elderly man who wore a permanent leer on his face. At closer inspection, it was clear that the literature went perfectly with the facial expression of its keeper.

"Danish, French—and others," Richter commented. "Simply terrible, isn't it, Sturmbannfuehrer?"

"Contemptible foreign trash," von Stadt replied, but his eyes clouded over as they stared at the display.

"Anything particular you look for?" the proprietor asked in broken German. "We got everything."

Von Stadt straightened to stiff attention. "The officers of the Reich do not have the morals of rabbits! Isn't that right, Hauptmann?"

"Disgusting, yes, sir! I agree!"

"Depraved, Hauptmann, utterly depraved. Look there, the one with the great whip. Do you suppose she could possibly enjoy it?"

"Probably, sir," Richter replied with a faint smile. "But I suspect she would much more enjoy the strong tool of a manly Aryan instead. A manly Aryan *officer* . . ."

"Yes. I . . . agree, Richter . . . yes."

At the next stall they visited, von Stadt was in for another surprise. It wasn't surprise in the goods displayed —rows of open crates containing a variety of exclusive alcoholic beverages—nor in the fact that the proprietor was a tough-looking young black man with a cigarette drooping from his lower lip. The surprise came when a door behind the stall opened, and a short gruff-looking individual in the uniform of a Russian air force lieutenant colonel came out and pushed his way past them.

"Ah," von Stadt said, immediately putting aside his initial annoyance at the rude Russian and stepping toward the now closed door. "And what good things might we have in here?"

Richter moved to check the SS officer's progress, but the black man was swifter—both in placing himself between von Stadt and the door, and in drawing a chrome-finished automatic pistol. "No!" Richter said, whether to the man with the gun or to von Stadt or to both wasn't quite clear.

"It's all right," Richter said, speaking to the black man in German.

"It's far from all right," the black man replied in the same language, his eyes on von Stadt, his gun remaining pointed at the Sturmbannfuehrer's lower stomach. "He doesn't have an appointment inside."

Richter moved to the side of the two men, taking in with a swift glance the expression of shock on von Stadt's face. "What I meant was he simply has made a mistake.

83

This is his first visit here. He merely thought there might be something of interest inside there. Is that not correct, Sturmbannfuehrer?"

"Yes, yes," von Stadt said as he allowed Richter to pull him two steps back from the gun barrel. "I was merely curious," he explained to the black man.

"You almost were merely dead," the black man said. But with a nod, he slipped the gun back into his jacket and smiled. "Check over the liquor, though. Prices for Scotch start at—"

"Later, perhaps," Richter said. He guided von Stadt away from the stall.

"I don't understand," the SS officer said. "What was behind that door?"

"Not what, Sturmbannfuehrer—who. A trader sitting at a table with a phone and maybe something else. It would depend upon whether his visitor was making an initial visit to arrange to buy or was coming to collect something previously arranged."

"A trader—in what, Hauptmann?"

Richter stopped and looked at the other man. "You name it. Secrets, mostly. Plans of planes and weapons under development. Troop movements or detailed maps of military installations. Psychological profiles of enemy commanders. Those sorts of things, and more."

"I don't understand," von Stadt said, eyeing Richter suspiciously. "Who would provide these things?"

Richter smiled. "Sturmbannfuehrer, I know this is all new to you, but you must realize that not all people are as loyal to their nation's war efforts as we are to the Reich's. Anything can be sold here that has a market. Secrets of any kind usually have a market. Thus, secrets are brought here by men whose only guiding principle is that of making a personal profit. There are men like that, Sturmbannfuehrer."

"Yes," von Stadt said thoughtfully. "I suppose there are."

"But of course, not in the Reich."

"But . . . of course not," the SS officer said, nodding slowly as if to himself.

"Come, Sturmbannfuehrer, let's give you the opportunity to use some of those chips you've received for your marks: Perhaps you can win enough to buy a retirement estate!"

Back in the hangar with the blue door, von Stadt's first three plays at the roulette table inside the marvelous gaming room were all winners. "A fantastic place, Hauptmann—fantastic!"

"You have said that before, Sturmbannfuehrer. But you are doing very well. Perhaps this is your lucky day —oh, one minute."

Von Stadt looked up to see a young man with his brown hair in a crew cut approach the Hauptmann and whisper something. Richter nodded and the young man went his way.

"One more play, Sturmbannfuehrer—then we have to meet someone—Mr. Percival Bellows."

"I understand that you have been remarkably fortunate at my roulette table, Herr Sturmbannfuehrer."

The speaker, seated on the other side of a table that a seventeenth century Spanish furniture-maker had crafted to accommodate at least twenty guests, was huge, at around three hundred pounds, with a somewhat piggish face. He had the look of a cruel and cunning bull boar. The black bristles of his cropped hair looked as effective as boar-tusks for goring an unsuspecting victim. The flat snout seemed alert for detecting the slightest trace of fear or weakness. The black dots of eyes pierced the very soul itself. Only the man's lips were out of piglike character; thin, bloodless, they parted minutely as the wheezing voice spoke and chilled the marrow of those whose bones he chose.

"Herr Sturmbannfuehrer?"

"Yes, Mr. Bellows."

"Yes, what, Herr Sturmbannfuehrer?"

Von Stadt's eyes sought out Richter's for some kind of moral support, but the Hauptmann was looking straight at

Bellows. Both German officers stood together on one side of the long table. There were no chairs in the room except for the ornately carved chair that bore the fat man's bulk. Those summoned to this room were not expected to remain very long, and if they did, Percival Bellows was not a man who cared overmuch for their comfort.

"Yes—indeed I have been fortunate."

"You have a familiarity with roulette?"

"Familiarity?" Von Stadt did not quite understand, even though Bellows's German was flawless. "Familiarity?" he repeated.

"What I refer to is skill with a formalized mathematical system that allows one to beat the table odds. Do you employ such an unsavory system, Herr Sturmbannfuehrer?"

"I should say not."

The black eye dots all but disappeared in their closing slits. "But if you knew such a system—if you did, Herr Sturmbannfuehrer—would you use it? Would you use it in my establishment?"

Again Richter was of no help—he simply wouldn't look at von Stadt. "The point is, Mr. Bellows, that I don't have such a system, so I am naturally at a loss to speculate—"

"You are not at a loss, Herr Sturmbannfuehrer. You clearly have left my table a winner."

"I did not mean that. No. What I meant—" von Stadt began irritably.

"Sturmbannfuehrer von Stadt means," Richter interrupted, "that, while his luck was fully with him during his short time at your wheel, he is well aware that in gambling the odds are always with the house. That being so, he also is well aware that, in all probability, he would have lost his winnings had he continued to play. He did not continue to play, Mr. Bellows, because we were told you wished to see us."

Von Stadt was sure his thumping heart could be heard in the uneasy silence. Percival Bellows finally spoke.

"Well said, Hauptmann Richter. If your reflexes in flying match those of your thought processes, you are doubtless a credit to your Luftwaffe. But you are inaccurate in one minor detail. You said 'us.' You said I wished to see both of you. That is not correct. I wished to see only one of you."

Von Stadt could not help but admire the way Richter stood his ground. "If you recall, Mr. Bellows, what I said was that I was told you wished to see us—both of us. My statement is totally accurate."

The silence this time was short.

"My man may have erred."

"He may have. However, now that the mistake has been clarified, I'm sure Sturmbannfuehrer von Stadt would not object to waiting outside."

"No objection at all!" von Stadt said in what was an explosive exhalation. "Perhaps I shall return to the roulette table, where perhaps I might lose a part of my winnings, maybe even all of—"

"No!" Bellows said.

Von Stadt swallowed. "No?"

"No. Hauptmann Richter has jumped to the wrong conclusion. Hauptmann Richter must learn to be careful about such presumptuousness. It is you, Sturmbannfuehrer von Stadt, with whom I wish to converse. It is you, Hauptmann Richter, who may return to the gaming table."

The eyes of the two German officers met. One set shifted uneasily. The other seemed to comprehend. Richter nodded and turned to the seated man.

"Mr. Bellows, this is the Sturmbannfuehrer's first visit here."

"I know that."

"Also know, then, that my commanding officer warned him about speaking to anyone here about anything—anything at all."

"That was very wise of your Major Koenig. Did he not, however, mention that there was an exception?"

"Major Koenig had no way of knowing that you would wish to speak to our guest in private."

"Major Koenig is not all-knowing. He is—as you are Herr Hauptmann—a guest here. My guest. As host, I have some prerogatives. I'll not detain your Sturmbannfuehrer for very long. Goodbye, Herr Hauptmann Richter."

"Goodbye, Mr. Bellows."

"Goodbye?" von Stadt repeated.

"I'll see you at the tables, Sturmbannfuehrer," Richter said. And then suddenly he was gone, and Bellows was smiling.

"Whatever else you may think, Herr Sturmbannfuehrer, I am a businessman. I wish to discuss business with you —business that can be mutually beneficial, as all good business should be. You do agree to that premise, I presume?"

"Well; yes. I suppose I do."

"Good, very good. Then let's get right down to the matter at hand. The industrial diamonds."

The SS officer wanted to sit down. Badly. The bones and tendons that held him upright had somehow exited with Hauptmann Richter. But there was no seat.

"Diamonds?"

The fat man's mouth moved into what von Stadt thought might be a smile. "I didn't think you would want to discuss the diamonds with Hauptmann Richter in the room. I am correct, am I not? To be specific, I doubt seriously that you have ever mentioned the industrial diamonds to the good Hauptmann—or, for that matter, even to Major Koenig. Am I right?"

"I'm afraid, Mr. Bellows, that I don't know what you are talking about." Von Stadt hoped that his expression showed a mixture of outrage and astonishment.

"Let's not engage in verbal byplay, Sturmbannfuehrer. You know perfectly well I am referring to the industrial diamonds for which you assume responsibility tomorrow evening. You are to ensure that the industrial diamonds get into the proper hands. I am suggesting that the proper hands in this instance are mine."

"Yours? But I—how do you know about—"

"I have many sources of information. One of them has told me that you will be taking charge of a large shipment of industrial diamonds tomorrow evening. Another source tells me that the British are in dire need of those diamonds for their armaments manufacture, and that a very handsome price will be paid to whoever is successful in handing them over."

"The British?"

"Why would I not sell them to the British? They, after all are my employers—British Intelligence, specifically."

"British Intelligence?"

Again the lip movement that might have been a smile. "I see. Your Major Koenig and Hauptmann Richter did not bother telling you the details of the situation at our cozy facility here. That is perhaps wise but I think you should understand my role. This base and everything that takes place here is a result of my suggestion to certain British Military Intelligence higher-ups that such an establishment would pay large dividends in their information-gathering mission. And I assure you they have not been sorry for taking my suggestion; they have received much value for the operational costs. Of course, what information they receive is also expensive. I and my traders are very accurate at assessing the worth of the goods we sell. Now, sometimes, the British think the price being asked is too high. The goods, in those cases, go to anyone willing to meet our price. And that is very profitable for me.

"But, coming back to your diamonds, yes, I'm certain the British would pay a good sum for them. But your side also needs them, I'm told. Therefore you and I might just hang onto them for a bit—to see who the higher bidder will be. After all, I'm in this war business only for profit—my own. Naturally, my supplier would profit handsomely as well."

"You and me? You want me to have the diamonds brought here? To you?"

"Is there something wrong with that arrangement?" Bellows seemed to think about his own question, then answered it. "I see, yes. The logistics of getting all those —how many boxes did you say there will be?"

"Two, but they are very heavy and—" Von Stadt

swallowed hard. He shouldn't have said that, but the fat man's eyes were almost hypnotizing in their effect. The Nazi shook his head to clear it.

"Two," Bellows repeated thoughtfully. "And very heavy. Yes, I can see your problem. But to Percival Bellows, problems are challenges—and other people's problems are opportunities. Very well, I'll take them from you on your own ground. Or I should say my representative will. Do you want the half-million reichsmarks in gold or silver bullion, Sturmbannfuehrer?"

"A half-million! . . . Mr. Bellows, I really cannot—"

"Exactly what is the problem, Sturmbannfuehrer? I'm sure you are not one of those fools like your Major Koenig and Hauptmann Richter—straight line, follow-the-leader sort of people, loyal to the end, both of them. Oh, there are plenty of such people—on both sides of the war. But you and I, Sturmbannfuehrer, we are different. We understand what life is all about. We are men of the world. Surely you consider yourself superior to these puffed-up peacocks of Luftwaffe fliers, do you not?"

"Well, certainly that's right, but—"

"Of course you do, and rightly so. When this war ends, just what do you think men like Koenig and Richter will gain from it all? A few medals at the most. Deserved, no doubt, but hardly negotiable. But you, Sturmbannfuehrer, you can leave your military service a very wealthy man —even if your side should lose the war."

"Lose? Unthinkable!"

"Probably so, but unfortunately the other side feels the same way. One side must lose, that is certain. But as for you, it does not matter now; you can win, whichever side loses. The world is your country. Now, let's get on to the arrangements."

"It—it is not that simple, Mr. Bellows! If the shipment were—ah, diverted—yes, diverted. If it were, I am the only person who could cause it to be so diverted."

"You mean diverted from the route the truck—I assume the carrier is a truck of some sort—is supposed to take? Yes, I fully understand. But suppose, just suppose, that before the shipment was to move out by road, you received orders from a superior. Orders which told you to divert the shipment."

Von Stadt shook his head. "No. You see, there is a code word. In order to change the route of the truck, I must be ordered to by someone first speaking that word. No enemy agent could trick me into diverting the shipment. Only my superiors who know the code word can command me, you see."

Bellows smiled again. "And who are those who know this code word?"

"In the Lisieux area, only myself, although the officer in the truck will know just before he departs—in case he must be rerouted while on the road."

"And you are authorized to tell no one else?"

"No one."

"Not even Major Koenig?"

"Definitely not!"

"Oh, that's too bad. You see the point I'm driving at, Sturmbannfuehrer? If you were authorized to mention the code word to Major Koenig, and then, tomorrow night when the shipment is diverted to a place where—well —something happened to it, then you could direct all suspicion of guilt to the Herr Major. Obviously the Major, not expecting that suspicion would fall his way, probably would not make certain his movements tomorrow night were completely verifiable. In fact, I think I could arrange it so that we could make sure of that. It's short notice, but I'm certain I could. Does the Major have a woman?"

Von Stadt laughed. "A cripple—and he has her for her money. And you think he's a fool. He's given me the same story about taking care of oneself now for afterwards, after the war is over."

"Well, then, he's right for our purpose. Yes, I think I can divert the Major's attention and place him in what will afterwards be an unverifiable spot. What's the code word?"

"The . . . ."

"Code word. Naturally, I shall need it—if my people are to avoid unnecessary bloodshed at the Lisieux end.

What I'm saying is that you carry out your operation just as you've planned, and with the code word, my people can take care of the transfer simply, easily. What is it?"

"You—you don't need it, not now! Just have your men call me at my office tomorrow. I have to think about this."

Bellows looked at his watch. "You have fifteen seconds, Sturmbannfuehrer. After that you will depart my office. Then I may or may not have someone call you at your office. If I do not choose to have him call, you are out a half-million marks in gold. If you do not care about that, fine for you—live in poverty. Fine for me, too; there are always other profitable endeavors for me, more than enough for the little time I have to consider them. But if you choose to be a part of this, if you choose to enrich yourself, you must tell Koenig the code word. That way he'll be forced to admit it under the questioning tactics of the Gestapo. That questioning might even be under your direct supervision. I'm sure you would enjoy that, yes?"

"I personally—"

"Never mind, I'm really not interested. Your fifteen seconds are over. The code word, Sturmbannfuehrer."

"Mr. Bellows—I—" Von Stadt struggled with his words. Then he fell silent and stared vacantly at Bellows.

"Is it then goodbye, Sturmbannfuehrer?"

"But—I—cannot simply reveal such a secret. No, sir, I —I cannot! Mein Gott!" Silence.

"It is goodbye, Sturmbannfuehrer. Perhaps, when you've had time to think about it, you will be more receptive to my man's call—if he calls. Goodbye, Sturmbannfuehrer."

Percival Bellows took a deep drag on his freshly lit cigarette and stared at the closed door for a few seconds. Then he picked up the telephone, pressing the farthest left of the four buttons on the receiver. When the answering voice identified itself, he asked to speak to John King. There was a short pause, and then he spoke, in English:

"I'm sorry, John. I accomplished very little." He repeated the essentials of his conversation with von Stadt, then added: "This puts me out of it for now, but if you or one of your squadron wish to play the role of Percival Bellows's man on the continent, you've got that option. But I hope you have a fall-back plan to get the code word."

He listened to John King's alternate strategy. Then: "Fair enough. I would make a suggestion to heighten von Stadt's faith in you, if Freddy will go along with it. It will cost him an airplane, but compared to industrial diamonds he's got plenty of those, right?" Bellows explained his suggestion.

There was a short discussion on the other end, which was swiftly summarized to Bellows.

The fat man laughed. "Tell him to stop acting like an old lady. He must have an old flying tub around somewhere he can spare. Hell, if he doesn't, I'll sell him one—cheap."

Chapter 9

Sunday, 15 June

It was 4:35 p.m., and the Messerschmitt had been in the air exactly fourteen minutes. Hauptmann Richter's eyes were busy scanning the sky above the soft but thick carpet of white cloud that formed an impenetrable floor between the fighter and whoever might be cruising in the sky below. Occasionally his eyes flicked to see how von Stadt was doing. So far, von Stadt was doing fairly well, for the 110 had been flying smoothly. So far, all the Sturmbannfuehrer seemed to have on his mind was a sense of relief to be gone from British soil plus a sense of accomplishment in his ability to trade in his gambling credits for two cases of Scotch whiskey and some pornography he thought no one else had noticed. He hardly looked green around the gills at all; but that would change, if things went according to Koenig's plan.

"See anything yet?" The Major's voice came over Richter's headset.

"Nothing. Maybe Uncle Freddy couldn't find a volunteer."

"You think he asked for one?"

"First time around, maybe. Hold it—we've got company. Five o'clock, up from the clouds. He sees us. He's closing."

"Nightingale here," Koenig's voice crackled in English. He was taking no chances. "This is Nightingale, repeat Nightingale. Anybody out there listening?"

"Listening, Nightingale," came the answer. "I gather you're the chap who's going to finish off this clunker once and for all."

Clunker was a good word for the aircraft, Richter agreed. It was a Hurricane Mk 1 that had seen quite a bit of combat duty. Judged by its battle-scarred and patchwork appearance, it had apparently single-handedly defended English territory during the Battle of Britain and had been shot at—and hit—by every German plane involved during the long months of that siege. The thought crossed Richter's mind that the machine might simply fall out of the sky before it could be shot out of it.

"Thanks for the help," Koenig was saying. "How do you see the action?"

"I'll call my shots and you call yours. When you want me to catch fire, I'll do so—just name the moment. Then down I go in glorious flames—until I get under the clouds. Then I hit the silk, as the Yanks say."

"You've done this before?"

"No. How about you?"

"A first for both of us."

The English pilot laughed. "You can paint a kill on that machine of yours. I hope this damned chute opens. Say when."

"When. Good luck."

"Ditto, old chap."

"Enemy plane!" Richter shouted at von Stadt.

Von Stadt had been thinking hard. About the fat man, Bellows. About what the fat man had said. About the half-million marks in gold bullion, and about the call that might—no, would come. And then what?

What would von Stadt do? Would he tell the agent the

code word? If he did, he'd have to tell Koenig, too, but that part would be easy. He could say that the diamond operation was so critical that he had to make sure that someone other than himself knew the code word—in the unlikely but possible event that something happened to himself. Yes, he could say that. But should he?

If Himmler ever found out . . .

But, just as Bellows had said, Koenig could be framed. Koenig would reap the trouble, while he himself would reap the benefits. But would Himmler appreciate the reasons his man in Lisieux gave as to why he thought it best to confide in Koenig? He might. After all, it was Himmler himself who just in the past week had suggested that the SS and the Luftwaffe work in harmony on this Falke business. Yes, he might not be able to argue at all.

But, no. Von Stadt was thinking logically. He knew enough about the Reichsfuehrer to realize that Himmler did not always think so logically when something went wrong—especially something as important as this crucial diamond shipment. The Reichsfuehrer would immediately be looking for a convenient head to chop off, and it might be that he'd not give his Lisieux Sturmbannfuehrer time enough to point to the party who really should get his neck severed. Or, it might be that Himmler would see fit to chop both heads. That certainly was in the realm of the possible.

On the other hand, there was that half-million in gold! And the possibility that Himmler would be overjoyed if he could criticize Goering's judgment in his selection of Staffel commander—for such a *special* Staffel.

But on the other hand, Himmler could do all that and still mete out severe punishment to his own man. Yes, he might have von Stadt shot—or worse—as an example of the kind of justice that Goering should deal out to Koenig.

Still . . .

He had but a fleeting glance at the other plane in the sky before the sky fell—or, rather, the ceiling came down and the floor took its place. His arms flailed until his hands found something to grip—

Again the sky turned upside down and the universe

within the 110 cockpit began sliding, shaking and rolling. Again von Stadt's stomach tried to explode upward—or downward, or sideways. He tried praying, but it was no use. . . .

Once more the aircraft jarringly righted itself and von Stadt heard chattering gunfire followed by a cry within the cabin. The Hauptmann had left his rear gun and was leaning forward, his eyes fixed to a point over von Stadt's left shoulder. "Look there, von Stadt—we've got him!"

Craning his neck, the SS officer looked out. His eyes widened and a surge of hope went through him, turning swiftly into jubilation. The Tommy plane was no longer coming for them. The enemy aircraft was wobbling in the air, hurt. And then von Stadt saw the flames coming from the front of the plane. It hung in the sky for a moment, as if time had stopped. Then, nose down, it plummeted. Down it went into the clouds, spinning, flaming. Von Stadt blinked, and all that remained in the surrounding sky to remind him of the dogfight was a thin trail of black smoke.

"We did it!" His cry was high-pitched, hysterical, lost in the din of the fighter's engine. He stretched out his arms to Richter, wishing nothing more than to share the moment of triumph with the other individual who had endured the terrible ordeal. But the Hauptmann lurched backward, as if repulsed by something, as if trying somehow to draw himself up into his face mask. Why?

And then the sharp acid stench bit into von Stadt's mind, and he looked down at himself. His uniform was completely, utterly soaked with the remains of lunch and breakfast.

He gagged again, but there was nothing more his stomach could contribute. With a shaking hand he reached toward the case of Scotch.

Von Stadt downed a burning swig, then another. They had done it! Fantastic! Exhilarating! He almost wished he had joined the Luftwaffe instead of the SS. Almost, but not really. The SS was where the real power was. A flyboy was a flyboy and that's all. Glamorous, certainly, but no flyboy will have any influence after the war is over. The SS now

. . . He drank deeply. This Scotch was hot and good, heady stuff.

Von Stadt looked up to see a grinning Hauptmann leaning down to him. Richter handed over a headset and motioned that he should put it on. Von Stadt fumbled off his leather flying helmet and slipped on the auxiliary earphones.

"Well, Wolfgang," Richter's voice crackled, "how did you enjoy your first victory in the air?"

Von Stadt laughed enthusiastically. The whiskey had easily caught him on his empty stomach.

"Fantastic! Fantastic, Herr Hauptmann!" He chuckled again. "Exciting! Almost as exciting as the spring of '36 —but I was just a young fellow then, and anything would have been exciting, even burning down that little Jew town! This was much better, Herr Hauptmann, much better. The speed, the sounds—all much better than watching a few dirty Jew shacks burn down.

"But tell me," he continued in all sincerity, "don't you miss seeing the enemy fall? I mean, there's something special in that, and you really miss that from up here." Von Stadt did not realize there was no answer from Richter, who was glaring with anger at the back of the SS man's bobbing head.

". . . something special, you know," von Stadt bubbled through his euphoria. "Why I remember that night in '36 like it was yesterday! There I was, with the flames and the searchlights and all those people running, half-naked—"

Richter switched off von Stadt's communications. He spoke to Koenig. "Major, do you still know how to barrel roll?"

". . . and me and that heavy machine gun . . .," von Stadt continued, oblivious to anything but his memories.

Suddenly, the fighter spun like a wild corkscrew, whirling round and round. Von Stadt shrieked in terror, clawed at his face and his head. The Messerschmitt tumbled him about like a rag doll, and von Stadt screeched again and again and again and again. But now there was no one listening.

"Herr Major!" Feldwebel Stumpf saluted. He had not liked the swaying motion of the wings as the 110 had come in. Still less did he like the swaying motion and general condition of the SS officer who was slowly descending the ladder from the cockpit to join the two unperturbed Luftwaffe officers already on the ground. But SS officers were none of the Feldwebel's business. The condition of the plane, however, was.

"Feldwebel," said Koenig, returning the salute. "I would appreciate your giving the entire machine a careful going-over. Especially the rear assemblies. We had a little British interference coming back and something may have been slightly damaged."

"There was battle, Major?"

"Battle?" the eager Sturmbannfuehrer repeated. "Ha! The Tommies will think twice about attacking the cream of the German Luftwaffe again!" The SS officer was on the ground now, but he still swayed. The Feldwebel noticed the half empty bottle of whiskey clutched against the soiled jacket von Stadt wore.

Major Koenig seemed unaware of von Stadt and of his statement. "Also, Feldwebel, I would appreciate your having someone take the boxes in the rear of the plane to my own office. You will find that the interior of this machine will require a good scrubbing down as well."

"Yes, Herr Major!"

"Finally, Feldwebel, I am able to bring back something special for you." The Major took from his tunic a small parcel. It was wrapped in plain brown paper, but the Feldwebel immediately recognized the contents from its shape.

"The Major is too kind," he said, his eyes aglow, hardly able to wait for the small square parcel to change hands.

The Major turned to Hauptmann Richter. "Would you take the Sturmbannfuehrer and arrange to have him cleaned up? I trust, von Stadt, that you will be able to dine with us this evening."

Von Stadt looked at the Major and nodded emphatically. "They will think twice the next time, the Tommies will," he said in reply. "I must find Fräulein Dietrich and tell her of our fantastic victory! Fantastic!"

He did not see the narrowing of Hauptmann Richter's eyes.

Richter later went to the pilot's canteen, where a young soldier was working behind the counter. The Hauptmann ordered some bratwurst with tomato sauce and slumped wearily into a chair. He was tired from the long flight and dozed for a time. He started suddenly when the soldier bringing the food accidentally bumped into him, spilling the sauce and sausage over his flight suit. It was a mess, but Richter was too weary to scold the youth, who frantically hurried to the kitchen for a cloth to clean the bright red stain that covered the pilot's chest.

While Richter was wiping away the sauce from his clothes, the door to the canteen opened quickly and Elsa Dietrich entered. She gasped and raised a hand to her mouth when she saw him. She hurriedly crossed the room and knelt at his side.

"Oh my heavens!" she cried. "Von Stadt told me you were attacked and that it was terrible, but he didn't say you were wounded, Hans. Oh my heavens! You must get to the hospital! Hans!"

He was too surprised to say much. But a light came into his eyes. He slumped forward with a groan and crumpled from his chair onto the floor. Elsa whimpered and called for the soldier behind the counter. Already upset with himself for clumsily spilling the tomato sauce, the young soldier scrambled to them and began slapping Richter's face and hands. He babbled something about the doctor and crashed out the door. Richter moaned slightly.

Elsa was nearly frantic. She cradled his head in her lap.

"Why did you come here? Why didn't someone take

you to the infirmary? Oh, Hans, my poor Hans. Oh Hans . . ."

She sniffed. Then sniffed again.

She put her nose to the red slop on Richter's chest and sniffed once more. Her face soured. He opened one eye and groaned again. She stiffened and looked down at him with a scornful pout on her face.

"Will I live?" he said weakly.

She yanked away her leg cradling him, and his head banged hard on the floor. She stood up and barged to the door.

"Hey!" Richter shouted, lying on his back, his neck craning, his head off the floor. "You nearly broke my skull!"

She spun around and glared at him, ignoring the smirk on his face. "I should have known better than to think somebody like you could actually bleed anything other than cheap bourbon!"

Then she was gone and Richter sat up, grinning.

"Cheap bourbon?" he mumbled to himself and rubbed the back of his head. "Not cheap bourbon, honey. You sure don't know Texas boys. Now cheap moonshine . . . that's a possibility. . . ."

At 9:30 that evening, Elsa Dietrich extended the bottle of red wine to the SS officer seated at her right. "More Burgundy, Herr Sturmbannfuehrer?"

"Wine? More? Why, Liebchen, I really don't think I should—"

Koenig interrupted. "Of course, our good von Stadt will have more wine. And after you fill his glass, mine also needs a little attention. Yours, Herr Hauptmann?"

Richter shook his head no, his hand reaching for the half-filled glass of bourbon before him. He had said little during the meal, but now he directed his words to the SS officer. "You were telling us, Herr Sturmbannfuehrer, about your many responsibilities."

"I was?" von Stadt murmured. His eyes left the smiling face of the woman and looked across the table. It took a moment to focus on Hauptmann Richter. The dinner for four had been excellent—though at the present instant, with the table already cleared of the plates, von Stadt couldn't remember exactly what had been served. But it was indeed marvelous to be here with the lovely fräulein, even if it was only in the canteen. Just the one table was occupied this evening—a very private dinner. Later, perhaps, he might—no, he would—suggest to the remarkably attentive fräulein that they go somewhere even more private. Yes. He would. . . .

"You were saying, Sturmbannfuehrer," Richter said, "that you had a most important mission of security tomorrow night. One that you were very concerned about."

"Concerned?"

"Something to do with a shipment of valuable goods of some kind. And the secret code word that you wanted to share with the Major."

"Share with . . . oh, that. No, I am not sure I should share . . ."

Koenig seemed to be smiling. "You are right, von Stadt. If you did share your secret with me, and if something went wrong with your secret shipment, why, I could become a target for interrogation. No, Hauptmann, I have no wish to know this code word."

"That is good," von Stadt said.

"But—but I am interested in a professional way, you understand, in how you would use such a word. Or rather, if someone else knew it, what good would it be to him?"

Von Stadt laughed. "Ach, my good man, don't worry yourself about such troublesome matters of top secret espionage. Believe me, Herr Major, life is much simpler as an ordinary Luftwaffe officer. Ach, these weighty problems should never burden a man like yourself. It takes an SS officer, such as you see before you, to deal with intricate and complicated, highly secret subjects. Nein, my Major, let those who understand these things take care of them for you. Eh, Fräulein Dietrich? Surely you can well understand how an officer such as myself must endure the loneliness, the solitude—the passionate solitude, Fräulein —of some intimate, unmentionable, dangerously amorous

. . . ah, I mean adventurous . . . conspiracies. Eh, Fräulein? Ach, yes. I knew you would."

At 10:15, Richter looked at his watch. Only he and Koenig now sat at the table.

"I still don't like it," the Hauptmann grumbled.

"Our fräulein is talented in many ways, Hauptmann. She may not have to go so far with von Stadt as to—"

"Don't say it. I don't want even to hear it spoken."

The tension waned slowly in the silence that followed. Then Koenig said, "If you feel something special for the woman, why haven't you told her?"

Richter emptied his glass. "You limeys know about social distance. But America, the land of the free and equal, is not without its own social distinctions. You know all our backgrounds. And you should know that a blue blood from Boston and a nobody from Texas don't mix."

Again Koenig was silent, then: "I think you may be a bit hard on yourself. And your judgment on the fräulein may also be a bit hard."

The bourbon rushed to Richter's head and his eyes darkened.

"If he's hard on her, if he lays a hand on her—I'll—"

"You'll obey orders, Hauptmann. That's what you'll do."

The clock by Fräulein Dietrich's bed said 10:30. Sturmbannfuehrer von Stadt, naked but for his undershorts, sat on the edge of the bed, his knees and feet together, his back straight as if he were at attention. His eyes were halfway closed, his breathing slow and regular.

He looked disgusting—was disgusting, the woman corrected. She stood before him, wearing only a bra and panties, both trimmed with black lace. The situation was now fully under control, but there had been a few moments earlier when it had been nearly out of hand. Immediately after the door to her room had closed behind them, von Stadt had made a savage grab for her. Fortunately, her hip toss sent him flailing and landed him on the soft mattress without his head colliding with the wall. An unconscious von Stadt would have been a problem.

"Wh–what happened?" he asked, pushing himself up to a seated position.

"You tripped," she replied. "Sturmbannfuehrer, we are going to have a very pleasant night together—I promise you we shall."

"Yes," he said, licking his thin lips.

She reached for a magazine on the nightstand and, opening it, showed it to him. "Hauptmann Richter took this from the airplane today. He said you purchased it in England. Is that true?"

Von Stadt swallowed hard. "Well, I . . ."

"Do you like what they are doing in this picture? Would you like it done to *you*? Perhaps by me?"

"Fräulein! If . . ."

"Well, then, that's exactly what we'll do. First, though, I want to show you something." She took the circular silver medallion from around her neck. "Do you like this, Sturmbannfuehrer?"

"I am sure it's very nice, but I cannot see it too clearly. You are swinging it too much."

She continued to allow the glistening silver medal to swing from its chain like a pendulum. It swung rhythmically, steadily. "You're not looking, Sturmbannfuehrer. Please look, I really would like your opinion. Look closer. Focus . . . That's right . . . Very good . . ."

Elsa Dietrich remembered what the old gypsy woman had taught her in Czechoslovakia; she let the flickering pendant soothe von Stadt, let it enfold his mind with its steady swinging back and forth. Back and forth. She had taught hypnotism before the war to friends at Vassar, but then it had been a parlor game. Now, it was deadly serious. Back and forth. Back and forth. Rhythmically swinging in von Stadt's slow eyes until they became blank.

When he was under her control, Elsa commanded that he deepen his trance state. Then she told him to focus his eyes on the magazine she had shown him earlier.

"This is what we have done together tonight. You will remember it very clearly. We both enjoyed it very much."

His head slowly nodded. "Yes."

"You were very clever in talking me into it. You were masterful in your persuasion. I was submissive and completely dominated by you."

"Yes. I was masterful. Yes, masterful."

"Excellent. Now, Wolfgang, we have no secrets from each other anymore."

"No."

"That is good. No secrets. That is why you shall tell me the code word. We have no secrets between us, and therefore you can tell me."

"Yes."

"You must not tell anyone else, but you can tell me."

"Yes."

"What is it then? The code word."

"Brilliant . . . the diamonds . . ."

"I am sure they are. The code word."

"Brilliant. I am . . . brilliant."

"I fully agree, Wolfgang. But what is the code word?"

"Brilliant."

"The code word is 'brilliant'?"

"Yes."

"Nothing more? Just the single word *'brilliant'*? Is that correct?"

"Yes."

"Thank you, Wolfgang. And now you shall forget that you shared this secret with me. You shall forget that I showed you my pendant."

"I shall forget."

"You shall remember only that we had a wonderful time together tonight, and that you were masterful in your persuasion. I was submissive and completely dominated by you. You shall remember in detail our time in bed together. A time just like in this magazine. You were masterful."

"I was masterful."

"When I snap my fingers you will awaken. We just will

have started putting on our clothes. You will tell me not to be frightened, that I have no reason to be afraid."

She stepped back from him and inhaled deeply. Now came the real moment of truth.

Feldwebel Stumpf was seated on his bed behind a bolted door and drawn blinds. He too was in his underwear, his enormous bulk free to ripple and shift according to the whims of gravity.

On the Feldwebel's lap was a distinctive box, the lid of which had been carefully placed on the blanket beside him. His face seemed lit from within by a combination of religious ecstasy and unholy greed as his eyes flickered over the ornate cursive script on the lid. The Feldwebel spoke very little English, but his pronunciation was perfect as he read the words softly, worshipfully:

"Prince Albert's Imperial Mint Creams. Selected for the Nobility."

His thick fingers entwined themselves in anticipation. Selected for Feldwebel Stumpf! Selected personally by the Herr Major, whose secret missions into English territory frequently resulted in the Feldwebel being given a box of Prince Albert's noble mints! Ah, life was so good, so very good! Within the box balanced upon his knees was a veritable treasure. His fingers eagerly and lovingly opened the green foil to reveal the flat discs of dark bittersweet chocolate filled with crackling layers of brittle mint, sandwiched with smooth white cream. Ah, life was truly very, very—

Suddenly his head lifted as if someone of authority had issued a sharp word of rebuke. No one had spoken in the silent room, but there was nonetheless a weighty presence. From the single photograph on the wall opposite the Feldwebel's bed, accusing eyes focused on the box he tenderly caressed—a box whose contents were made by the Reich's mortal enemy!

For a long moment the Feldwebel seemed to shrink under that ominous gaze, then he carefully placed the box on the bed alongside its cover and moved timidly to the wall and its glaring photograph. This too had become part of the ritual, an unpleasant part to be true, but a necessary one. With eyes averted he lifted the photograph from its nail and returned it to its place, face toward the wall.

"Forgive me, mein Fuehrer," the Feldwebel whispered, closing his eyes and turning back toward the bed. When the eyes opened, they were again filled with lust.

"Feldwebel Stumpf!" The bellowed command rattled Stumpf out of his revery and caused his fingers to tremble. He dropped the first mint to the floor. He gaped at the back of Hitler's picture in awestruck fear.

"Feldwebel Stumpf!" The voice crashed into his fuzzy senses. But it was not the scream of Der Fuehrer. Oberleutnant von Spiegel was shouting to him from beyond the closed door and down the corridor of the barracks. Stumpf struggled clumsily into his trousers and lumbered to the door while still closing his flailing buckle.

"Stumpf!"

"Ja, Oberleutnant! I'm coming!" He yanked the door open, stuck out his head, and peered down the dim corridor to see von Spiegel standing at its far end, his flying scarf dangling rakishly from his shoulder. "Ja, Oberleutnant! What is it?"

"Stumpf, there's a leak in a fuel tank. I was strolling in the main hangar just now while looking for Buergermeister Gruff. The fuel is running out steadily. One fool with a cigarette could blow the whole works up in a moment. Get some boys together quickly, will you? It's got to be drained or patched tonight!"

"Ja! Ja! Herr Oberleutnant! Thank you, sir!"

Stumpf looked in confusion down at the empty chocolate wrapper in his fingers. He grunted and sucked in air. Gasoline leak! The main hangar! Ach! He wavered between going back into his little room or rushing off after von Spiegel. Churning frustration rose within him, and he dashed back into his quarters, snatched up a shirt, dragged out three mints, unwrapped them hurriedly, and stuffed them into his mouth as he ran out the door. The wrappers dropped in the corridor, leaving a trail behind the frantic

Feldwebel who raced off to fetch his men. The door to his room was left ajar.

A few moments later, soft clopping steps came down the corridor. They stopped at each mint wrapper. Square teeth sampled the foil. Nibbled. And gobbled them up contentedly.

One wrapper after the other disappeared. Then Buergermeister Gruff paused, head cocked, nose flaring at the smell of sweet chocolate that wafted from the Feldwebel's darkened room. Tentatively, Gruff pushed forward, and the door creaked open. He poked in his head, stepped into the room, and had no trouble at all finding the Prince Albert Imperial Mint Creams littering the rumpled bed.

"But, my dear—"

"Please, Sturmbannfuehrer—please just go. I don't want to see you—for a while, at least. Please!"

"But there is no reason to cry. Don't be afraid. You have no reason to be afraid. Please, Fräulein—er, Liebchen—we had such a good time together."

Her eyes were red, her face wet with tears. "I . . . I couldn't control myself. You were so . . . so . . ."

"Masterful?"

Chapter 10

Monday, 16 June

The Countess von Coburg placed her teacup back onto the table beside her wheelchair. It was 11:40 in the morning, and the cup had been filled twice already, as had those of the two men who shared the divan in the mansion's sitting room. She had listened patiently as the Luftwaffe Major had explained his plan to intercept the shipment of industrial diamonds. It was an excellent plan, simple and decisive. She granted him that, and so did the white-haired man in his seventies who had been the picture of thoughtful patience as he examined the Major's map and its markings.

"To sum up, then," Koenig said, "the plan depends on us intercepting the truck and using the code word on the officer in charge of the shipment. We'll order him to take the truck on a convenient detour, and then the diamonds shall be transferred to our own vehicle."

"And the German guards?" the old man asked. "They'll recognize you."

Koenig nodded slowly. "We'll have to kill them, Pierre."

The old man said nothing. A leader in the local maquis, the Frenchman was not troubled by the prospect of death for German soldiers.

"Once the diamonds are in our hands," Koenig said, "we'll get them back to the Staffel base and then fly them over to England the next morning."

The old man stood up from the divan and began to pace thoughtfully. Then he said, "Your attack plan is fine, although you may have trouble shadowing the truck without detection. But, even without that difficulty, my friend, I must tell you that the plan requires extensive revision."

Koenig suddenly was on his feet. "What?"

"Extensive revision," the old man said calmly. "Your plan is sound, based on the information the maquis have given you. However, that information is incomplete. You see, we have just learned that there are three trucks, not just one."

The woman spoke softly. "Our Sturmbannfuehrer von Stadt seems to be more clever than anticipated. All three trucks shall depart the railroad siding at the same time. All three shall carry boxes that shall be identical from the outside. All three shall take different routes. Our agents close to the Nazis believe they can discover the routes before tonight by watching the movement of SS patrols and by seeing where sentry posts are being established—very quietly—between the rail siding and the secret factories. But time is of the essence here, John. You must know which is the correct truck to attack. You cannot afford to strike the wrong one, for they will be expected to check in at these sentry posts at predetermined times. If one is late, the SS will be out in force. They know this is important and they will be at their most deadly. You must hit the right truck the first time."

Koenig sat down heavily and looked at Pierre. "How can we find out the right truck? Can your people get that information?"

Pierre shook his head. "Only von Stadt knows that. I'm afraid, my friend, it is in your hands. We can do little more."

"Your only hope," said the woman, "is to control the movement of the right truck from the very beginning."

Koenig thought of Percy Bellows. There was a chance —a slim one, but a chance. His eyes hardened in contemplation. The others in the room watched him in silence. After a few minutes, he got up.

"It's still possible," he said. "If the maquis can keep the Germans busy, and if von Stadt is a good Nazi . . ."

He said nothing about the dangerous threat of Himmler's falcon.

At 1:30 p.m., Leutnant Fritz Mueller rose out of the hard wooden chair and strode across the room, his hands clasped tightly behind his back. He had been in the waiting room for twenty minutes. Upon arrival at the Nantes air base, Mueller had delivered Goering's teletype directive and an order from Major Koenig to an Oberleutnant, who inspected both without emotion and brought him to this room. "Here you wait," he had said.

"Here I wait," Mueller had repeated. The room was fairly large, but furnished with only four wooden benches, two chairs, and a desk. One of the chairs was occupied, otherwise the room was empty.

"Here you wait also," Mueller observed to the young woman who occupied the chair.

She looked up from her book. "I am told that is what waiting rooms are for, Herr Leutnant," she replied with a smile. She was young—mid-twenties, the Australian guessed—and her figure was full without being overly so. Her hair was brownish blonde, her face . . . well, beautiful in a soft way. There was a slight suggestiveness about that soft look, but only slight. It was, Mueller decided, a virginal softness.

"What are you waiting for?" he asked.

Her shake of the head told him that it was none of his business. Her smile told him that she didn't mean to be rude. Her voice confirmed that fact:

"I don't suppose you would care to tell me what you are waiting for?"

"Correct," he said.

She smiled once more, then went back to her book.

Mueller was getting impatient. Fortunately, young German Luftwaffe officers were not known for their store of patience, so he was not particularly unusual in his restlessness.

His clicking steps took him to the far wall of the room, then he turned and strode back to his chair. He glanced at his watch.

"You are nice to look at, but you are much too tense. Don't you get paid unless you are actively doing something?" The woman's smile was back, her book temporarily set aside.

"I would like to get back to my base, Fräulein—or is it Frau?"

"Fräulein—Fräulein Renate Haas. And you?"

"Fritz Mueller."

"And your base is where?"

"Lisieux. I'm here to fly someone back there."

"And you now await this someone."

"Yes, and you?"

"I await someone, too, Leutnant. Of course, my waiting has not been as suspenseful as yours, since I know who your someone is."

"You . . . ?"

"I am called Falke. Yes. Shall we go now to your aircraft?"

The Me-110 had the sky to itself on the return trip. The pilot, however, did not have his thoughts to himself. The girl, obviously familiar with aircraft interiors, had placed the mask and headset over her face, and now was using the communication radio. Mueller gave only curt replies to her comments. He was still confused by Falke being a woman—a beautiful woman.

"You don't seem to like me very much, Leutnant."

"I don't like you or dislike you, Fräulein Haas. That's not part of my mission."

"It's my mission you don't like, then. I have met officers like you before. You don't like spies."

"Spies are necessary."

"They do save German lives, Leutnant."

"I am not looking for an argument, Fräulein."

She sighed. "Maybe I am. Maybe I would like someone to try to talk me out of my mission."

"That," he said, "would not be very patriotic of me, would it?"

"I suppose not. What do you know of me, Leutnant?"

He answered carefully. His experience during his first day at Lisieux had taught him to be careful of his tongue, and for that enlightenment he grudgingly thanked Koenig. "I know that you are said to be very good at what you do. I also know that the Reichsfuehrer himself has ordered your current assignment. As is quite obvious, I know very little else about you. Oh, I assume you have a good command of the English language, since England is where we're taking you."

"And your English, Leutnant. How is your English?"

"I can say *good morning*." But Mueller said it so it sounded more like the German equivalent.

She laughed. "Keep practicing. Within months, you'll be able to order a complete English breakfast."

"And I'll get an Irish stew with ravioli."

"You have a nice sense of humor, Leutnant. That is rare these days, at least in the circles that I travel."

"How does one earn the name of the falcon?"

"One earns, in my profession, Leutnant, by doing what one is told—and by surviving. As for the name, it pleases certain people to give those they control such dramatic-sounding labels, regardless, I might add, of their physical presence or their accomplishments. For example, I could introduce you to a colleague of mine who wears thick spectacles and has the stature of an underfed but overgrown ten-year-old boy. Professionally, he is an accountant. His code name is Stingray."

It was the pilot's turn to laugh. "It is a very strange war," he said.

"It sometimes is a very sad war, Leutnant."

"Yes."

For minutes, only the throbbing dual engines of the Messerschmitt filled their ears. Then:

"You still don't like me, do you, Leutnant?"

"Fräulein—"

"Don't say anything, please." There was an almost desperate edge to her voice, as if she were about to break into very real womanly tears. "Please, I want you to understand. I don't know why, but I—I want to tell you something about me, something I will flatly deny, if you dare repeat it on the ground or try to accuse me with it. I will flatly deny it."

"You don't have to tell me anything, Fräulein."

"But I must! I . . . Why, Leutnant, do you think people—ordinary people—suddenly become involved in my line of work?"

"There's glory in it, for some, I guess. That's one reason."

"Then," she said, "there also is a desire to further the victory of the Reich. There is loyalty to the Fuehrer as well. And, in some cases, there is a full measurement of sadism. In my own case—"

"I repeat, you don't owe me an explanation."

"I want to tell you—somebody—no, you! In my case, I have a younger sister. She is my only living relative. She lives in Köln. She is married to a musician. He is a very nice man, a very loving husband. He is also a Jew."

The Leutnant swallowed hard. "And those in authority learned of this?"

"They learned. And they gave me a choice." Her voice cracked, then as it spoke again, hardened just a trifle: "And you, Leutnant, what do you think of the choice I was given—and the choice I made?"

He watched his words carefully. "I . . . have no thoughts about either, Fräulein. A Luftwaffe Leutnant like myself is involved in a different kind of war . . . a totally different kind."

* * *

It was 6 p.m., and Major Koenig's face was cold with fury. His eyes burned holes through the man who stood before his desk.

"Damn it, von Stadt, you said nothing about your agent being a woman!"

"Really, Koenig, I did not believe that to be of any importance." The Sturmbannfuehrer was suppressing a smile. For once he had managed to rile the stolid Luftwaffe Major, and he clearly was enjoying himself.

But Koenig was not. The day had started off badly, and gone into a steep dive from there. After his return from the disconcerting meeting with the Countess, he had seen von Spiegel, who had taken the news about three trucks with a lack of emotion that put Koenig in an impatient mood. Shortly after that conference had ended, along came the SS officer von Stadt to announce that, due to his very busy evening, he could not properly host agent Falke that night and therefore he had decided that Falke could remain on the Staffel base until tomorrow's flight to England. What in hell more could happen?

Falke could and did happen. When Koenig recovered from his initial surprise, he got an uncomfortable feeling about Leutnant Mueller, who had escorted the woman to the Major's office. Koenig asked von Stadt to escort the agent to Fräulein Dietrich and to arrange Falke's quarters with her own for the night. Then he took advantage of being alone with Mueller.

"All right, I'll spell it out, Leutnant. You're to continue as the little lady's escort. Stay with her like glue. We've got enough problems trying to slip in and out of here tonight without being watched by a trained spy."

"All night?"

"Is there something you don't like about that prospect? She looks as though she might be a good night's entertainment."

"Listen, Major, you've got this woman wrong."

Koenig sat back, leaning his chair against the wall and lacing his fingers behind his head. "Have I? Have I got one of Himmler's trusty cutthroats wrong? Tell me about it, young Herr Leutnant."

The Australian told him what Falke had said about her Jewish brother-in-law. "It's not her fault," he concluded. "And now you're asking me to make love to this girl, knowing full well that tomorrow we'll betray her as a spy?"

"Correction, Leutnant. I have not asked you to do anything. I have ordered you."

Mueller stiffened. "Is there anything else Herr Major has to command?"

"Yes, Leutnant. At the front of the main hangar there is a night-light which normally is not in use. I trust you will be awake at one-thirty in the morning. If at that time you notice that the light is on, it will mean that my mission tonight has failed. Shortly after that time—as shortly thereafter as you can manage—I suggest you climb into one of our aircraft and get the hell out of here."

Mueller had stalked out of the office as stiff as a starched shirt; not long afterward von Stadt returned. In the interim, Koenig had given the matter of Falke concentrated thought. There was a real risk that Leutnant Mueller, feeling the way he seemed to about the agent, might inadvertently give something away. On the other hand, the fact that Falke was female was an advantage. A male spy couldn't be kept occupied in the manner he intended for Falke. Nonetheless, he wished he knew more about her. Himmler would not normally entrust an important mission to the kind of girl that Mueller was convinced she was. When von Stadt came in, a smirk still on his face, Koenig decided on a strategy to find out who Renate Haas really was.

"Damn you, von Stadt! You should have told me the SS was sending a woman!"

"Now, Koenig, really, you must be reasonable about this. Are not both sexes involved in our glorious mission of victory for the Reich? Take Fräulein Dietrich, for example. Does she not serve?"

"She serves—but not as a combatant."

Von Stadt smiled, thoroughly enjoying his advantage. "She is not at all bad in combat, that is in certain kinds."

Koenig stood slowly, threateningly—at least that was the impression the movement made upon the SS officer. "We are not discussing Fräulein Dietrich, von Stadt! We are discussing Fräulein Haas—who will not be flying to England tomorrow in one of my planes—"

"Not fly—"

"You did not allow me to finish my statement. The next word was to be 'unless.'"

"Unless what?"

"Unless, Herr Sturmbannfuehrer, within the next two hours I have upon the surface of this desk your file on this Haas woman. If the material in that file does not satisfy me as to the professionalism of this innocent-looking girl whom you chose to call an effective professional agent, I will call off my part in our joint operation. I naturally will inform Reichsmarschall Goering of my reasons. I am willing to face any consequences. He, in turn, will inform Reichsfuehrer Himmler of my reasons, one of which will be the lack of cooperation and frankness on the part of the SS—especially the lack of communication with regard to the sex and other particulars of agent Falke. Do I make myself clear, Sturmbannfuehrer? I am endangering my relationship with Percy Bellows. And, my friend, so are you. That is not good. Bellows must not have doubts about Falke, not if we are asking him to slip her into England through his secret base."

A withering sneer hardened over the SS officer's sallow face. "You speak very rashly, Major, of the consequences of disobeying the Reichfuehrer's commands. But no matter. It's your neck, my friend. . . ." Von Stadt shrugged his shoulders. "You shall have the information you seek," he said coldly. "I for one have no desire to fall out of favor with Herr Bellows. Not at the beginning of such a promising acquaintance. You shall have the Falke file."

* * *

"Young Mueller will get his first real test tonight," Richter said and drank his ersatz coffee. He sat at the counter in the base canteen. The door to the canteen was locked, because Elsa Dietrich sat across from Richter, composing a coded radio message asking for the help of Percy Bellows. She finished, silently read it over once, and prepared to retire to her room in the rear of the low building, where a shortwave radio was concealed in a false wall of her closet. She looked back quickly at Richter and spoke:

"Bet you wish it was you instead of Mueller who was supposed to manhandle Falke tonight, eh?"

She tried to smile, teasing, but the joke fell flat when she saw Richter's dark scowl. He downed the rest of his hot drink and stood up.

"Don't look so insulted, Hauptmann," Elsa tried to soften her comment. "It doesn't become you."

He stared with accusing eyes. "She's no more my type than von Stadt is yours."

Her eyes dropped, and she shuddered involuntarily at the memory of last night. Then she smiled at him and said softly, "I'm glad you give me that much credit, Hauptmann."

He looked intently at her and nodded. "I do, Elsa."

She flushed a little. Smiling again, she sighed and waved the coded message weakly, then went through the door leading to her room and locked it behind her.

Strange, thought Richter as he left the canteen and stepped into the warm sunshine. She somehow seemed grateful for what he had just said. Maybe she wasn't such a hard-boiled Bostonian after all.

In her locked room, Elsa closed the curtains, and the chamber became dim. She opened the closet door and switched on a small bare bulb. A panel that was cut into the wooden closet wall came down flat, revealing a small radio set. Its workings quickly glowed to life. She put on a set of headphones, sat down at a chair in front of the radio, and prepared to send the message across to England.

But, for a brief moment, she thought of Richter. It was surprising that he looked so indignant at her misguided jibe about him and Falke. But it was nice that he understood the ugliness of her night with von Stadt. She flicked the switch to "send," and felt a lift of heart that had not come to her since those happy days living in Czechoslovakia before the Nazi invasion. Perhaps Richter wouldn't always be so eager to spend every spare minute chasing French girls. Perhaps. That would be something, wouldn't it?

Von Stadt had just inserted a cigarette into his long ebony holder when the telephone rang. It was his private number. Always, he disliked answering the private telephone. Always, the voice on the other end of the line would have something questionable to say. Not all that many people knew the number, and most of them were individuals of much importance. And most of them shouted threats instead of talking in a friendly manner.

The phone rang again.

The day—this important day of all days—was going from bad to worse. He had been haughty with Koenig this afternoon until the flyboy pet of Goering decided to exercise his prerogative about not flying Falke until he'd read her file. Just minutes ago he had sent Klemm to the Staffel air base with those papers—another humiliation. And now—

The phone rang again.

Crushing the unlit cigarette into the yellow alabaster ashtray on his desk, von Stadt picked up the phone. "Ja?"

The voice sounded weak, as if it came from a long distance. "There is a code word, a certain word having to do with tonight's operation. You have the intelligence, I trust, to have remembered it—is that correct, von Stadt?"

Without realizing it, the Sturmbannfuehrer had risen and now stood at frigid attention. His mind made a precipitous leap, and a vision of a man sharpened and faded. The voice belonged to Percival Bellows.

"So, my dear Sturmbannfueher," the voice said cheerfully. "As I said it would, this most profitable telephone call has at last come to you. And now, if you will tell me that word which I requested at our last meeting, all that I promised shall be arranged within the week. Of course, you have only my word as security, but, as you must know by now, there is honor among men such as you and I. You can trust me. In fact, you must, for you have no other choice. You must trust me, Sturmbannfuehrer, because if you refuse to cooperate, you shall die."

Von Stadt swallowed his breath. He gasped for air. Bellows went on, but now his voice was soothing, placid.

"My dear Wolfgang, let us not trouble ourselves with such distasteful . . ."

"Nein!" von Stadt shrieked hoarsely. "Nein! Nein! I shall never betray the Reich! Never! No matter how much you offer me, I shall never betray the Reich!"

It was silent except for von Stadt's labored breathing. The SS officer listened for some response from the other end of the line. Nothing. He slowed his breathing, slumped to a chair, but still held the receiver hard against his ear.

"Mein Herr?" von Stadt asked carefully. No answer. "Mein Herr, does this mean I shall never be permitted to return to your magnificent base in England? Mein Herr, surely you must understand . . ."

Soft chuckling. Soft, amused chuckling came over the telephone line. Von Stadt listened as the chuckling turned into a steady, rippling laugh.

At last, Bellows said: "Congratulations, Sturmbannfuehrer. Congratulations, Wolfgang. You have passed the test." An astonished and confused von Stadt waited for an explanation, which came after another long wave of jovial laughter.

"Yes, Sturmbannfuehrer, you have indeed passed your first test. Congratulations from all of us in the Service. . . ."

"The Service? . . ." Von Stadt was frantic. He wished he could at least placate this international intriguer enough to return to the secret base. But what was this congratulations all about?

"Yes, yes, you have passed this most critical of tests of your loyalty to the Reich, Sturmbannfuehrer, and your success shall not go unrewarded. Your success, Sturmbannfuehrer, was . . . *brilliant!*"

"*Brilliant*? Did you say? . . ."

More laughter. Then Bellows said, hardening, "Brilliant! Indeed, Wolfgang, I said 'brilliant.' That is the appropriate word to use at the moment, is it not? Yes, Sturmbannfuehrer von Stadt, this secret is no longer entrusted solely to you. I share the responsibility with you."

The weight of this revelation sank into von Stadt, and his confusion drained. Bellows! Bellows knows the code word! Bellows is an agent for the Reich! Bellows!

"And now, Wolfgang," the voice was cold and formal once more, "listen carefully to what I have to tell you. For the sake of the security of this shipment—not to mention the security of your present rank in the Service—listen carefully. I am your superior in this mission, and I have been instructed to inform you that the shipment of diamonds is in great jeopardy."

"Jeopardy?"

"The maquis know of your plans. They know of the three vehicles, and they intend to intercept them all. But there is a way whereby you, von Stadt, can take advantage of the situation and deal a decisive, crippling blow against them. You shall reroute the shipment tonight, transferring it along the way to another truck, as I shall specify for you in a moment. Then you shall send a force of motorcycle troops behind each of the three decoy trucks at a distance which shall keep them out of sight of the ambuscade yet shall give them enough proximity to counterattack and inflict heavy losses against the maquis. Understood?"

Von Stadt jumped to his feet and clicked his heels in eagerness. "Understood, Mein Herr! It shall be done!"

What a magnificent chance for von Stadt. A chance to outwit the maquis, deliver the industrial diamonds safely, and redeem himself to a man of power and influence, Percival Bellows. Magnificent! Von Stadt listened carefully to the specifics of the plan and assured Bellows that his orders would be faithfully carried out.

Von Stadt hung up and rubbed his hands together. Now he could get down to more immediate business and rid himself of that pack of French peasants he had imprisoned in reprisal for the factory sabotage. Ach, but these trivial day-to-day matters took so much valuable time from an administrative officer! Especially now, when there were diamond shipments to protect and maquis leaders to outwit. Ach! Such drudgery at a crucial time like this!

The tension of waiting until the mission began that night gnawed at Hauptmann Hans Richter. Major Koenig was busy with last-minute details for the diamond heist, and it was Richter's job to keep Feldwebel Stumpf and the rest of the loyal German ground crew involved with aircraft maintenance and out of Koenig's hair. Richter strolled away from the hangar where Stumpf and his grease monkeys were busily overhauling a Junkers 88 dive bomber recently assigned to the Double Cross Staffel. The sun was comfortable, but it did little to burn away the uneasiness that settled on Richter when he considered that the Staffel's security might be jeopardized if any of its members were killed or captured on tonight's mission.

Then, someone was walking at his side.

"You're deep in thought, Hans," said Elsa Dietrich. She looked fresh, slim, and very appealing this afternoon —not at all the way the Texan imagined a chilly Bostonian would look. He returned her smile.

"Thinking about tonight?" she asked and looked at the ground.

"Certainly am," he said. They spoke German.

"Me too," she brushed against him. "Please be careful." her voice dropped to a whisper, "David."

He half-turned to her and she caught his eyes with her own. "That's just what I was thinking," he said, and grinned.

They walked quietly. Now and again their casual movements brought them together, lightly touching shoulders. Conversation was halting; then there was none. They found themselves behind the hangars near an area overgrown with brambles and weeds, which had once been used for small arms target practice.

"How is your wound?" she asked, and her eyes twinkled.

Richter rubbed the back of his head. "I think you really did break it."

"You deserved it."

He chuckled. "It was worth it."

She gave him an elbow, but he slipped it past, and she fell against him. To her surprise, his arms were around her and she was looking up into his open face.

He spoke gently. "Ginny, I'm sorry you had to go through that last night."

She moved closer to him and whispered, "David . . ."

"Hauptmann!" a voice bellowed cheerfully. "Ach, Hauptmann, there you are! I've been searching all over for you, Herr Hauptmann! Heil Hitler!"

"Feldwebel Stumpf," Richter sighed, and Elsa stepped back, absently patting her hair.

"Begging your pardon, Herr Hauptmann, but as Herr Major Koenig is not available, I must ask you, sir, for your recommendations on how to handle a matter of repairing the control linkage of the Junkers. There's a weakness . . ."

While Stumpf babbled dutifully on about the repair, Richter glanced at Elsa, who was wandering away.

"Ah, whatever you think best, Feldwebel," Richter said to the mountain of human flesh bobbing before him.

"Ja, ja, Herr Major. As you wish. I shall . . ."

While the Feldwebel chattered on about alternative ways to do the job, Richter was looking at Elsa Dietrich, who turned once to him, then strolled down a path leading to the woods nearby.

". . . which one do you think is best, Herr Hauptmann?" Stumpf asked intently.

"Good idea, Feldwebel," Richter mumbled, and walked after Elsa. "Do it that way."

"But, Herr Hauptmann . . ."

Richter was already hurrying to the shadowed opening in the trees where Elsa had disappeared. Stumpf shook his head and clucked his tongue as he lumbered around to go back. "Always, the responsibility for such decisions must fall on the shoulders of the enlisted man. He's a good flier, that Hauptmann, but he has no idea of how his machine works." He clucked his tongue again and waddled toward the hangar.

Richter caught up with Elsa as she crossed a brook on an unsteady log. She balanced shakily in the middle, her arms waving. He called to her, and, distracted for the moment, she faltered and slipped off the log into the knee-deep stream. He stumbled into the water and caught her before she was drenched. Richter laughed as he picked Elsa up and strode across the brook with her cradled in his arms. He set her down on the mossy bank where the sunshine filtered warm and green through the trees. He lay beside her. They did not talk.

The sounds of the gurgling brook and the sweet short melodies of birds in the trees stopped time. Richter's face came down to hers, and she touched his cheek lightly with her fingers. He brushed her brow with his lips. . . .

"Herr Hauptmann! Yoohoo! Herr Hauptmann! Ach! Verdammt bushes! Ach! Yoohoo, Herr Hauptmann!"

The woods shook and rustled with the crunching approach of Feldwebel Stumpf. Birds twittered and darted away. Elsa and Richter sat up straight. He swore in English and stood up to see the red-faced, puffing Feldwebel burst from the thickets across the brook, wheezing and yoohoo-ing with every step.

"Ach, there you are, Herr Hauptmann! Ach, begging pardon, Herr Hauptmann, but I must have your signature on this form authorizing the work you suggested a moment ago. Here . . ." The Feldwebel held up a clipboard in one hand and a pen in the other. He stood, heaving from lack of breath, on the opposite bank, looking uncertainly down at the ten-foot log spanning the water between them. He smiled wanly, looked down suspiciously at the log, and then back at Richter with a pleading look on his chubby face.

"Stumpf, can't that wait?" Richter asked, annoyed. "No? Well, then come over and I'll sign it."

Stumpf forced a smile and looked with furrowed brow at the log. He placed one tentative boot on the end and licked his lips.

"Ach, Herr Hauptmann," he said and chewed his back teeth. "I, er, that is I'd be grateful if you . . ."

"Come over or go back. That's an order!"

"Which . . . er . . . which is an order, Herr Hauptmann? Come over or go back?"

"Take your choice."

"Choice? But . . . this form must be signed by the Herr Hauptmann, Herr Hauptmann, before I . . . can . . ." He stepped solidly, heavily on the wobbly log. His tongue stuck out the side of his mouth. He glanced uneasily up at Richter. Both feet were now on the log. He inched forward.

Exasperated, Richter turned to look at Elsa, who was sitting primly at the edge of the stream, tossing broken sticks into the water and watching them float away into the darkness of the woods. He shook his head and watched Stumpf, edging, edging, breathless and red-faced, across the log. He was nearly halfway. . . .

"Feldwebel . . ."

"Ja, Haupt . . ." Stumpf should not have been so soldierly. Forgetting himself, he snapped to rigid attention, and like a felled tree, keeled backwards. He thrust out one bulky leg, yelped a passionate appeal to his Maker and crashed into the stream.

Elsa Dietrich threw her hands to her face and ran off into the woods. Richter, restraining hysterics, pinched himself on the cheek and climbed onto the log to reach Stumpf, who was soaked completely from boots to garrison cap—except for the work-order form and the fountain pen, which he held triumphantly above his head.

"They're not wet, Herr Hauptmann!" he proudly announced while lying to his chest in the cold water.

Richter chewed his lips and walked out to the middle of the log. He reached down for the clipboard and pen. With a flourish, he signed his name and handed the pen and paper back to Stumpf, who heaved to his feet like a weary elephant and waded back across the stream.

Richter dashed off down the path after Elsa. But before he got far, Stumpf's urgent voice hounded after him. Richter, expecting a waterlogged Feldwebel who could not scramble up the bank, raced back to the log crossing. On the other side, the sheepish mechanic stood with downcast eyes, dripping wet.

"Well?" Richter demanded.

"Herr Hauptmann," Stumpf said with apologetic motions of the hands holding the pen and clipboard. "Herr Hauptmann, begging pardon, but you must also sign the second copy underneath."

"Damn! Damn!" Richter complained, as he debated whether to rush after Elsa and ignore Stumpf. Then he decided against it. "All right, damn it, Stumpf! Stay there! I'll come to you! Damn it!" He darted nimbly onto the log, crossed, and leaped to the bank next to the beaming Feldwebel. He snatched the papers and pen, scribbled his name quickly, and thrust them into the mechanic's fat hands.

"Now, don't bother me again! With anything!" He jumped onto the log, then twisted slightly and pointed a warning finger at Stumpf, who was making sure the signature was in order. "And I mean anything! . . ." But Richter was too confident. His foot skidded away, he gasped in surprise and splashed chest first into the stream. A shrieking peal of laughter burst from the trees. Stumpf caught his breath. He saw the Hauptmann was unhurt and was slowly getting to his feet, so with all the discretion learned from a lifetime in the military, Feldwebel Stumpf vanished.

Elsa's laughter came again, and Richter glared at her

delighted face, which popped up from behind a fallen log. The face disappeared, but the laughter rang once more.

Richter, still fuming, waded heavily out of the stream. He picked up his garrison cap, filled it with water, and walked idly toward the log where Elsa lay. He approached casually, even finding a tune to whistle. Just before he reached her, she looked up, curious. She saw the capful of water, shrieked "No!" and tried to escape. But he soaked her neck with the icy water, grabbed her shoulders and pulled her, laughing, shrieking, down to the soft grassy ground. Her laughing stopped when he kissed her. And kissed her deeply. Her arms pulled him urgently against her, and her hands gripped his wet hair. "David," she murmured.

After a breathless, blissful moment, Richter drew his face back. His eyes were gentler than she had ever seen them. Her eyes were more lovely than he had ever expected. He kissed her again, now without urgency, with tenderness, as though they had all the time they could ever want to fall in love.

Chapter 11

Monday, 16 June: 11:30 p.m.

"Hurry there! Be careful, idiots! Do not drop them!"
The short thick man in the black trench coat moved
impatiently along the rail siding between the open freight
car and the open rears of the three military cargo trucks.
He was directing the beam of his flashlight at several
uniformed soldiers who were working in pairs to lift and
carry six heavy wooden crates. Each of the crates measured
a foot square and three feet long and weighed close to
ninety pounds. Each crate was enough of a burden without
the additional problem of the trench coated supervisor
getting in their way.

"Klemm, get away from there!" von Stadt said.

Klemm immediately snapped to. He hurried to the
front of von Stadt's staff car, where the SS officer stood
watching the transfer. "These men are idiots!" Klemm
muttered. "How we allow men like this the privilege of
wearing the uniforms of the Reich is beyond my—"

"These men, Klemm, have managed to safely bring
this cargo to this point. They do not require your assis-

tance. Therefore, you will kindly remain here—with your mouth shut. Am I understood?"

"Jawohl, Herr Sturmbannfuehrer!"

Von Stadt left his underling and walked to the dimly lit rear of the nearest truck. Peeling back the black leather of his left glove, he glanced at his watch. It was 11:40 p.m. So far, so good. The night was dark and, except for the noise of the train's steam engine, there was a ghostly stillness about the lonely country landscape. He looked at the two crates now lying in the rear of the truck. In the light of his flashlight beam, they looked like two miniature coffins. He shrugged off the thought and concentrated on the numbers stenciled on the box ends. These bore the correct numbers: BR-1110. These contained the real cargo.

"A fortune, yes, Sturmbannfuehrer?"

Von Stadt nearly jumped out of his boots. The voice reminded him of Percival Bellows, but perhaps that was because the words had expressed the very thought passing through the SS officer's mind. But the young Leutnant in charge of the shipment bore no resemblance to that of the dealer in secrets and stolen goods.

"A fortune, yes," von Stadt agreed with the man.

"The trucks are loaded. My men and I will now reboard the train, if there is nothing else."

"Nothing else, Leutnant. You have done your work well. Heil Hitler."

"Heil Hitler."

As the train began moving slowly to the east, von Stadt walked around to the front of the truck, a Citroen two-ton model, like the other two vehicles. Two uniformed SS soldiers sat in the cab. "You understand your instructions?"

"Jawohl, Herr Sturmbannfuehrer," the driver replied.

"They are to be followed to the letter. There will be absolutely no deviation. None! Leave now."

"Jawohl, Herr Sturmbannfuehrer!"

When the last of the three trucks had departed into the night, the traces of their taillights winking out one by one around the turn of the roadway, von Stadt stood silently looking about. The sound of the train had also faded. All was still. An uncomfortable place, he reflected. Shaking his head, he walked to where his staff car waited. Behind it were two other vehicles, a second staff car and a Renault two-ton truck, and a dozen soldiers waiting for orders.

"All goes well so far," Klemm said, as von Stadt approached.

"So far. Yes." His gloved hand stroked his pointed chin. "Klemm, have one of the men drive me back to headquarters. I want you to take the other staff car—and the rest of the men—and follow the route of the first truck. Then continue with it after it transfers the diamonds to the next truck. Later, when the French attack the decoy, wipe out the swine!"

Klemm's vehicles set off. Again von Stadt waited until no trace of the lights of the staff car and the truck that followed it was visible. As the soldier who had been detailed to drive his car opened the rear door for him, the Sturmbannfuehrer stopped and turned toward the night. An oppressive night. Haunting. A feeling . . . that he was being watched.

He was.

And in the trees on a hill two hundred yards to the east, the watcher placed field glasses into a battered leather case. Silently, the figure took from another bag a scarred walkie-talkie.

"This is Simone. . . ."

Tuesday, 17 June: 12:09 a.m.

The headlights of the Citroen truck with the industrial diamonds picked up the tail end of another vehicle parked in the road ahead.

"This is the right place," the driver said.

The other man in the cab thumbed off the safety of his machine pistol.

"It is the right vehicle as well." The truck ahead was a light Borgward B1000. On its left side was a hastily painted white crescent, sharp ends up. Reaching a point some three yards behind the Borgward, the Citroen halted, its motor continuing to run.

Two men stepped from either side of the parked truck and into the headlights of the Citroen. One was an SS captain. As he drew closer both men in the rear vehicle recognized him as the officer responsible for the next stage in the diamond shipment.

"Heil Hitler, Herr Hauptsturmfuehrer."

"Heil Hitler. Transfer the crates immediately."

Without a further word, the two men hurried to obey. At precisely 12:13 a.m. the two soldiers in the Citroen watched the Borgward move east from them. "I'm glad to be rid of those boxes," the driver said.

"I as well. I—wait! What is that?"

They were standing at the rear of their truck, having just closed the tailgate. In the distance, along the road they had just traveled, they could see lights. "A car—or a truck. Two sets of lights, I think."

"Let's get moving! It could be the French!"

It wasn't; it was in fact Klemm. But the man who suddenly stepped out from the bushes at the side of the road had known French from childhood. However, he decided German was more suitable to this particular occasion.

"Heil Hitler," he said, a sardonic grin on his face. Then, using both hands, he lobbed the two grenades he carried. This maquis was overeager to kill Germans, and his attack now endangered the mission. He dived for cover as the grenades went off, then fled before the soldiers in the truck following came on the scene.

"You are a very strong man," Falke said in a whisper. "I cannot remember ever having made love with one such as you."

There was but one small desk lamp giving a soft light to the room which had been prepared for the overnight guest at the base. The bed was not large, but it was a bed rather than a standard issue cot, and so the two had enough space.

Nor was there reason to be concerned about that at the present, so close did they press against each other.

"That is not the first time you've done that," she said.

"Done what?"

"Resisted looking into my eyes. Why don't you want to look at me—look into my soul? You did enjoy my body, did you not?"

"You are well aware that I did, Fräulein."

"Was I then too—too aggressive? I know that there are men who wish their bedmates to be tame as kittens."

She had been anything but kitten-tame. In the space of the past two hours, they had united three times. Each time she had transformed herself into a wild tiger. There was an urgency in her lovemaking—a desperate need. It was the need of one who knew there might not be another time, there might not be a tomorrow at all. In the past, Mueller had felt that same kind of need himself, but not with such an overwhelming totality. Perhaps, then, it was the spark of life within—perhaps this soul within the woman knew that tomorrow she would be . . . No, he corrected himself. Tomorrow had already become today.

"Your thoughts are far away," she said softly.

"I'm sorry."

"You are thinking of home? Where is that, Fritz?"

He hesitated. "I do not think of my home at all. I wish not to speak of it."

"You have your own secrets, then?" She smiled. "It's all right, my iron man. Keep your secrets. I am not working at my profession this night."

Neither was he, he thought. The others were out there in the night somewhere, risking their hides, while he . . .

Her fingers began to move downward from his chest. "Do you think, my man of iron, that we might . . . perhaps one more time? . . ."

He smiled, more at himself than at the woman. Whatever the others were doing, no one could argue he wasn't doing his bit for the war effort. "Since you put it that way, Fräulein, I consider fulfilling your request in the nature of a patriotic duty."

* * *

The bottle of Scotch the Sturmbannfuehrer had just opened crashed to the floor beside his desk. "They did *what*?"

Over the hand radio held in von Stadt's trembling fingers, Klemm's voice repeated the message: the first truck that carried the diamonds had been blown up just after transfer. He feared the truck with the diamonds now was in danger, for the attack on the first truck had come sooner than he had expected.

"Why were you not there, you bumbling fool?" von Stadt screeched. "Get after the diamond truck immediately! If anything happens . . . Get after them!"

Von Stadt bit his black-gloved finger harder than he intended. He swore and threw the radio against the far wall of his office. He gripped his throbbing head with both hands. "Mein Gott! Mein Gott!"

Then von Stadt regained his composure. His shrewd mind calculated, craftily judging the possibilities. His head still throbbed, but he took control of his thoughts. He began to pace the room, back and forth. The shipment was surely to be intercepted. But where?

He hurried to the wall map of the district, and with a shaking hand he traced the planned route of the truck. There! He tapped the spot, the spot the clever maquis would choose for ambush if the truck were to be taken before the SS could catch up with it. Yes! That would be the right spot. He contemplated the map a moment longer, then knew what he must do. A motorcycle patrol was close enough to set up a roadblock at the far end of the trap. With Klemm and his men coming up the other end . . . Yes, that was it! He had them!

Von Stadt slapped his hands together and ran to pick up the radio. But it was smashed beyond use. He swore and rushed out of his office in search of another one. He would outwit these maquis after all. He'd finish them this time. They would run right into his hands, and he would snuff them out at last!

At 12:20 a.m. the SS officer sitting in the righthand seat of the Borgward carrying the diamonds pulled his Walther P38 from its holster.

"There—in the road."

His driver had been pushing the truck to nearly fifty kilometers per hour, the maximum it could do and still be controlled on the narrow, twisting roadway. Now, in his headlights, he could see the tree that had fallen across the road. No, not fallen—not in this place, not on this night. He slammed on the brakes.

"Turn!" the officer ordered, realizing even before he got the word out that the driver had anticipated the command and was already spinning the wheel and downshifting. They lurched forward in their seats as the gears ground into reverse and the truck jumped backward. There was a thumping sound on the door panel to his right, and as the change into the forward gear jerked his head back against the top of his seat, the officer caught the glint of metal at window level. He saw the business end of a Luger. Then the night exploded before his face and he saw nothing more.

"Nein!" the driver screamed at the man standing on the running board near the officer. He never saw the gun that fired through his own window.

Both black-clad gunmen jumped from the truck as it crashed into the brush ahead. Then the man who had been on the driver's side reached in over the dead driver and switched off the engine.

"Quickly," Koenig said, already pulling the bolt on the tailgate.

Von Spiegel darted around even before the gate was down. The two men lifted the first crate of diamonds from the truck and hurried to the fallen tree, stepping over and through its branches. They half-ran to the vehicle waiting a dozen feet beyond. It was a medium closed-body Opel truck. The crate slid into the open rear door on the right hand side of the car.

"The other one!" Koenig snapped.

"Right. I've got the replacement parcel." Von Spiegel held up a shoe-box-sized package he'd taken from the Opel. When they reached the rear of the Borgward, he carefully placed the package inside. "Fair return is no robbery, quite!" he said.

"Let's get out of here," said Koenig.

They had just moved the second crate over the tree when Richter's voice came from the road before them. "We've got company, Major. Easy—no problem yet. Keep coming."

Both men had been about to drop their burden and go for their weapons, but now they continued their run to the Opel. When the second crate was inside the vehicle and the door closed, Koenig turned to see who it was that Richter was talking about.

She wore black trousers and jacket, a beret of the same color covering her short hair.

"What the hell are you doing here?" he asked angrily.

"You require help," she said.

"We seem to have had some unwanted help already. Who was responsible for the earlier fireworks?"

"One of my people who was too eager to kill Boche. He destroyed the decoy truck. Too soon, I fear," she said, and her eyes dropped momentarily before they came up again. She spoke with determination. "Von Stadt knows his plan is going wrong. He has set up a roadblock on this road to intercept the truck you just stopped. He wanted to make sure the goods got through safely after their transfer—with an escort of motorcycle SS."

"Where?" Koenig asked grimly.

"About two kilometers ahead. They might have heard your own shooting here, and they could be ready. At any rate, they'll stop all vehicles for inspection, and I don't imagine you'll like that."

Koenig quickly assessed the situation. To drive back the way the captured truck had come was impossible because of the downed tree and also because of the chance of more SS following. There was no choice but to take on the motorcycle barricade—to break through and make a run for it. Simone interrupted his thoughts.

"They have machine guns, but so do my people, who are in the woods near them, waiting our arrival. Then they'll open fire on the Boche. In the meantime, the other two trucks are being struck as planned, but the maquis shall be gone again when von Stadt's monkeys catch up to the decoys. We must depart. My people are impatiently waiting for us. . . ."

"Us?" Koenig stopped her as she moved away. Her dark, flashing eyes were steady on his.

"I have a car up ahead. I shall lead you through."

"You can't. You'll be . . . I won't have it! Our own car is armored!"

"You stole it from a military compound two hours ago, correct?" she asked bluntly.

"How did you know?" von Spiegel asked, surprised that his deft handiwork had been so quickly discovered.

"The maquis sometimes know before the Boche Ober-leutnant," she said, and almost smiled. Then she turned to a pensive Koenig and said, "The car shall be recognized immediately by this squad of SS, I assure you. You'll never get close enough to break through without someone else distracting them first. And that's my place, John."

"Simone," Koenig grasped her arm as she began to turn away. "You can't do this! There's no reason you have to—"

"I have good reason," she said grimly. "You know who blew up that factory." She paused to let her words sink in. "Today von Stadt's men murdered fourteen villagers. Executed them—" Simone's voice caught, and she fought back a sob. In a whisper, she said, "They were my people, John. I'm going now."

Simone began to run swiftly up the darkened road, then stopped. From the dimness, she called, "Lights out. When we get to the top of the hill, turn your motor off too and coast down behind me. When you see my lights go on, start your engines and . . . and I'll see you for dinner tomorrow evening, John. Six sharp. And don't be late!"

She faded into the night, leaving the three men staring in admiration.

"That's some woman," von Spiegel said.

Richter nodded. "Pray she remains in one piece."

"Let's move," Koenig said. "There's more company coming, and they're not friends."

Richter and von Spiegel looked back down the road at the dim lights approaching in the distance. "Right," von Spiegel said. "Let's go meet our welcoming committee!"

"Halten!" Klemm shouted to his driver as he jumped and ran from the car before it skidded to a stop. The tree in the road . . . and there, the truck! He motioned to the truck following the car. "Hurry, we must check the—"

At that instant, von Spiegel's replacement parcel blew the Borgward into a collection of vehicle parts and turned Klemm's world upside down.

"She's going to crash through a roadblock driving that?" Richter said. He was at the wheel of the armored Opel. Koenig was in the right front, cradling the Erma MP 38 submachine gun, the barrel nosed out his window. In the rear of the enclosed car, von Spiegel steadied an identical weapon and trained it to the left to cover the driver's side.

Simone was driving a small Volkswagen sedan—a civilian car with nothing in the way of protection.

"I don't believe it!" Richter said.

"She's going to try, believe that," Koenig spoke through clenched teeth. "But the element of surprise is in her favor."

Richter was about to say something about the odds of survival being small, but decided against it. Koenig, after all, had been the one to lecture him on the valuable role of women in war; now let him ponder his own advice.

The lights of both vehicles were out, but if their motors were heard approaching, the SS motorcycle patrol would be ready. The element of surprise Koenig spoke about lay in the fact that the awaiting Germans had chosen the bottom of a steep hill for their reception. The strategy of the two vehicles was to cut their engines at the top of the hill and freewheel down the decline as far as possible before being discovered. Then—one hoped—the engine would respond when the clutch was engaged and the accelerator jammed to the floorboards.

As they watched the Volkswagen ahead begin the upward climb leading to the critical downward stretch, von Spiegel gave voice to the thought that Richter had declined to speak. "You know why she's doing this, Major?"

"I know."

"You're a lucky man, John."

Koenig's face was a mask of grimness. "She'd damned well better be a lucky woman."

"Here we go," Richter said. The Volkswagen was over the hump and lost from their sight.

"Shouldn't you try to get some sleep?" Falke asked.

"Yes, I guess I should."

"What is it that you are thinking about so hard? Me?"

"Perhaps."

"I am flattered. Will you think of me afterward? When I am in England?"

"Yes. Yes, I will think of you."

"That makes me happy, Fritz. I am glad to know that someone will think of me in a nice way. It *will* be in a nice way that you think of me, won't it?"

"Why wouldn't it be?"

"You've not used my name once. My first name, I mean. We have made love four times this night, and you have not once called me by my name."

"I apologize."

"Will you use my first name? Please, it is important to me. I don't know why it is important, but it is. This night . . . now. Please?"

"Of course . . . Renate."

"It sounds strange the way you say it."

"How so?"

138

"It sounds as if—well—as if it is a name you will never say aloud again."

"Perhaps it is because I am tired."

She laughed, but it seemed to Mueller that it was a forced laugh. "Yes, that I can understand. You should sleep, my darling. Otherwise you may not be able to keep awake when you fly me to England tomorrow."

"Today," he said.

"Today? Yes, you are right. Good day, then, close your eyes—until morning, Fritz."

"Until morning . . . Renate."

"Sweet, sweet Jesus!" Richter drawled softly in English.

His hands tightened on the wheel as the Opel went over the crest of the hill. As if his cutting the ignition and slipping the stick into neutral were a combined signal, the roadway at the bottom of the long decline suddenly burst into light in three places. Three French grenades exploded among the Germans, and their loud reports startled the three pilots in the Opel.

"Maquis," Koenig said. "Turn the engine back on, Richter—no need for secrecy now."

The Volkswagen ahead was already picking up speed, hoping to take advantage of the confusion the grenades had caused among the Germans below. The motorcycle blockade had been placed expertly along twenty yards of road. But many motorcycles had fallen from the grenade explosions. In the light of another grenade flash, the road appeared to be in complete disarray. Pieces of twisted machinery were flying everywhere; soldiers were running and scrambling into defensive positions, attempting to fire those weapons which had not been dropped in the first moments of the attack. And already the chattering of the SS guns had begun.

Richter switched on the motor of the Opel, jamming the gears and depressing the accelerator as far down as it would go. As he did so, Koenig and von Spiegel aimed their Erma machine guns to the front through the windows.

Below and ahead of them, the Volkswagen was roaring into the first edge of what had been the original blockade line. Immediately German guns began to turn from their targets in the dark forest.

"Faster, damn it!" Koenig's voice pierced Richter's ears, followed by the thumping of the Major's Erma. Von Spiegel held his fire. There was nothing either of them could hit at this distance. No doubt Koenig knew that as well, but he was desperate to do something, even if that something made no difference.

The night resounded with a bizarre orchestration of engine roars, machine gun poundings, and grenade explosions. Blinding light tore open the blackness. Richter strained his neck forward to see the road. Only a few moments more and they'd be right in the thick of the blockade.

"She made it!" von Spiegel shouted over Richter's shoulder. The smile of relief that began on Koenig's lips froze. The Volkswagen indeed had smashed its way through the motorcycles and had burst clear to the far side of the blockade, but a stream of flame suddenly shot out of the car's rear engine compartment. In an instant, the Volkswagen did an uncontrolled, high-speed dance in the roadway. Then it left the road and dived into the brush on the right. Two of Koenig's heartbeats later, a detonation shook the earth itself; the bright sheet of flame shot up and its reflection bounced down from the thick clouds above.

Almost immediately the flames shrank to become a gasoline-fed brushfire. Armed Germans were running toward the wreck. That distraction, in addition to the guns still firing from the blackness of the roadside, gave the Opel important unchallenged distance. By the time the German machine guns turned toward them again, the Ermas of the Opel were hammering viciously.

Other sounds began converging on the ears of the three men. A scraping crash of metal against metal, a thump and a short-lived scream, tires squealing in protest as Richter yanked the steering wheel first one way then the other, loud drumstick rolls on the metal of the enclosed cab, the clatter of glass as von Spiegel's Erma fired a hole through the rear window. He stuck the barrel through and opened fire. Again metal clanged against metal and there were several more screams as the front wheels rose up and over someone in their path and the rear wheels crunched the broken body into lifelessness.

Koenig jammed a second magazine into place and immediately began spraying the first of the thirty-two rounds in his front-to-side field of fire. Then, turning in his seat, he shifted the butt of the weapon to his left hand so that he could cover the rear of the car—the direction from which most of the enemy guns were now firing. As the fingers of his left hand curled around the grip, a glint of light bounced off the gold ring he wore on his fifth finger. His jaw muscles tightened and his eyes momentarily were drawn to the fiery wreck that only moments before was Simone's VW. At that moment an SS trooper came running toward them, his outline illuminated from the fire behind.

"You bastard," Koenig said through his teeth, and it was as if he and this man were all there were in the night, in the mission, in the entire war. With deadly aim and intense control that held the Erma on target in spite of the bouncing, rocking, swerving Opel, Koenig emptied the full magazine. The man went down gripping a middle section that now was only partially attached to the rest of him.

"We're through!" von Spiegel shouted from the back.

"Not quite yet," Richter said, switching on the headlights. "Look here."

Von Spiegel looked. Ahead of them was a single motorcycle, its rider hunched low over the machine as it attempted to outrace the car bearing down on its rear.

Richter could see the motorcyclist's frenzied eyes and horror-filled face as he turned quickly to gauge the swiftly decreasing distance from the careening Opel. So close were they now that Richter could see in the headlights the rank insignia gleam on the man's uniform lapels.

The Opel's bumper slammed into the rear of the motorbike. Bike and rider upended over the left fender of the car and rejoined the roadway behind it.

"He didn't salute, Herr Hauptmann," von Spiegel observed.

Richter's voice took on the tone of an officer of the High Command. "I shall require that man's name and rank, Oberleutnant. Have it on my desk in the morning."

"If you stop, I'll scrape the insignia off the fender right now."

Both men looked at their silent, still commander. He was looking down at his left hand—specifically, at the ring on his little finger.

Chapter 12

Tuesday, 17 June: 5:45 a.m.

"I do not wish to hear any more bad news!" von Stadt shrieked. "I wish to hear only good news!"

Klemm stood as stiffly as he could manage, considering that his right arm was dangling in a hastily applied sling. His clothes were strips of leather and rags. He was covered with dirt and encrusted blood—the result of the abrasions he'd received from his somersault and collision with the roadway after the explosion of the Borgward. His left knee was somehow not right in its joint, and his neck ached so badly he could barely keep his head erect. He needed sleep —or the comfort of death. Anything but von Stadt's remorseless assault.

Yet as bad as Klemm felt and looked, his commanding officer looked even worse. The Sturmbannfuehrer's eyes were red from the Scotch that stank up the office. His face was a landscape of nervous twitches and rivulets of sweat. To Klemm, he looked like a mad dog, one that needed immediate shooting. But this mad dog was the SS base commandant, and it was he who ordered the shootings—or worse.

Klemm had gathered the reports of the night's action as he had been ordered, and he had delivered them to von Stadt. He had anticipated the violent reaction of his Sturmbannfuehrer and had tried to soften the details. But it was not easy to soften them. The armored Opel had been found. But it was empty. The crates carrying the diamonds had not been found. Additionally Klemm had no idea how the maquis could have penetrated the SS plan.

"I did not even know the code word, Herr Sturmbann-fuehrer. To my knowledge, only you—"

"I said good news!"

Klemm thought for a moment. "Well, I checked the Double Cross Staffel air base."

Von Stadt's eyes seemed to brighten. "And? And *what*, you fool?"

"Well, at least Falke is off to a successful start. They're now in the air, heading for England."

"England . . ." Von Stadt repeated the word slowly. Something clicked in his head. A vision of sorts, two wooden crates . . . like miniature coffins . . . on the floor of a Messerschmitt . . . a plane marked with double crosses. Another vision, that of a fat man—a leering, terrifying fat man. The fat man's face faded, replaced by Koenig's. But Koenig didn't know the code word. Only von Stadt and Bellows knew it.

The telephone rang harshly, and von Stadt jumped.

It rang again, and he stared wide-eyed at it.

Eager to please, Klemm hobbled over and answered it. He looked at von Stadt, whose face was pale and close to shock. Klemm whispered, "Sturmbannfuehrer, it is a Herr Bellows."

Von Stadt's chin dropped. He struggled to compose himself. He took the telephone and said weakly, "Ja . . . mein . . ."

"Von Stadt, you are finished!" The voice was not angry. It was matter-of-fact, but icy.

"Ja . . . mein . . ."

"Finished, von Stadt, now that you have failed the Reich! Do you understand me?"

"Ja . . . mein . . ."

"Finished! Kaput! Unless . . ."

"Unless . . . unless *what?*"

"Unless I personally send a letter to Himmler exonerating you of fault in this disastrous failure. A letter which would be sent to Himmler through Goering by way of Major Koenig."

Von Stadt's strength was gone, but a faint glimmer of hope sparked within him. "Mein Herr, you mean you would do that for me?"

Silence.

Then slow chuckling from the other end of the line.

"Wolfgang, I must have a soft spot for your slow-wittedness. Yes, I shall send a letter through Major Koenig. I shall explain in it that the SS is not solely at fault in this matter, that circumstances were beyond their control, and so on. I presume that shall please Himmler enough that perhaps he'll not be so eager to find a head to lop, eh?"

"Y . . . yes, but . . . why would you do this?"

"Because, as it happens, Wolfgang—and this should be just between us, eh? As it happens, I have friends in the maquis, also. . . ."

"Mein lieber Gott!"

Chuckling, hearty chuckling. Von Stadt felt faint.

"Those diamonds have found their way into my own surprised hands." The chuckling began to grate on von Stadt's nerves. "I'll help you because in the future you may be of use to me. Next time, I expect you to cooperate from the start. I presume you have learned that lesson."

Von Stadt knew the omnipotent Bellows had duped him. He held the telephone in one hand and his aching head in another.

"So, for your sake, Wolfgang, let's just say the maquis won this little game with superior numbers, planning, and sheer good luck. I assure you, my connections to Himmler —and Himmler's reluctance to accept any embarrassing humiliation of his SS—shall see to it that the fate of this secret shipment of industrial diamonds shall in no way compromise your position at Lisieux." Cold, cold laughing. "Auf Wiedersehen, Wolfgang. Auf Wiedersehen."

Von Stadt hung up with shaking hands, both of them rattling the receiver in its place. Bellows had masterminded the theft but, ironically, von Stadt was in his debt. He would even be compelled to be grateful to Joachim Koenig, who would bring the message from Bellows to Goering. It was all quite distasteful, yes. But better than an SS firing squad.

Wolfgang von Stadt did not know just how badly the Double Cross Squadron and Percy Bellows needed to keep him in charge of the SS unit at Lisieux. At least von Stadt was a known quantity. Von Stadt would never ask whether there really was a letter from a Percy Bellows exonerating him from blame in the loss of the industrial diamond shipment. And there would never be such a letter, but Koenig would suggest to Goering that he blackmail Himmler with the evidence of the SS bumbling. Goering could offer to help cover up the SS failure in return for future favors from Himmler. At Koenig's prompting, Goering would suggest to Himmler that von Stadt be left as local SS commander. In that way, Koenig would tell the Luftwaffe leader, the Staffel could go about Goering's business without snooping from more dangerous SS officers.

Below the clouds was Occupied France. In the hazy light of the dawn sky, two Me-110s flew in rotte formation —the fighter occupied by Koenig and Richter was in the lead position, and the one piloted by Mueller was behind and slightly above. Both aircraft carried valuable cargo: Koenig's held the two boxes of industrial diamonds, and Mueller's bore Renate Haas, the spy code-named Falke.

Behind both 110s and higher yet, von Spiegel watched the skies from the cockpit of his Me-109. He had an uncomfortable feeling in the pit of his stomach this morning. At first he had dismissed the discomfort as simple physical and mental exhaustion. But the feeling was something more; it was a premonition. He tried to shake it off, but failed. Last night's run had been exhilarating, to be sure, but it had taken a heavy toll on all of them. Even Mueller, the Australian, looked as if he'd been through hell and back. Even so, he'd looked much worse after spending ten minutes alone with the Major just prior to take off.

The Major, no doubt, was feeling the worst of all. Von Spiegel shrugged. Hell, if rank has its privileges, it also has its payments due. No, that wasn't fair—not in this instance —not with the Countess gone. The hell with it all! One day, maybe, when the war was long over, he could sit back in a book-lined study somewhere with a crackling fireplace before him, a snifter of brandy under his nose, and then he could afford to philosophize about the deep meaning of it all, if there was such a deep meaning. For now he was simply a warrior. Simply. He laughed ironically to himself.

At the same moment, Mueller heard Renate Haas laugh over his headset. "Again, my Leutnant Fritz, you are silent. Is this the 'morning after' problem, or is it something more?"

Mueller's face relaxed. It had been set ever since he was summoned to Koenig's office before dawn. Koenig had gestured toward a chair. "How did things work out last night for you?"

The chair remained empty. "Fine, just fine," Mueller said tautly. "The condemned woman enjoyed a hearty roll in the hay just prior to the final betrayal that will deliver her to her execution."

"You are casting yourself in the role of betrayer?"

"What would you call it? You don't know this woman, Major. I've told you her background—the hold they have on her. Damn it, she can't be held responsible for whatever it is she might have done! I've talked to this girl. I've heard and sensed what's broiling inside her. Yes, I feel I'm a betrayer, Major! I think you would too, if you knew of her what I know."

"Do you have any suggestion to make, Leutnant?" Koenig had asked. "Before you answer that question, though, I'd like to read something to you. The file on my desk comes from von Stadt. It is extremely classified information, but he had his reasons for letting me see it.

I'm sure he wouldn't fully approve of my sharing it with you, but perhaps he would appreciate my desire to impress upon you the highly efficient nature of the members of his branch of service. I suggest you sit, Leutnant."

Mueller had taken the seat, but not until Koenig was well into his reading.

" 'Renate Haas, also known as Maria Meinsdorff, also known as Ulrica Netsen and five or six other names. Current code name: Falke. Fluent in German, English, French, Dutch.' Let me hit just the highlights of her service—the various commendations from her superiors. Let's see. 'Infiltrated French Resistance line moving downed flyers home; responsible for information leading to execution of eighteen men, women, and children on this mission.' Here's another: 'Successfully obtained information on secret Dutch codes, thus leading to capture and execution of—' "

Koenig looked up from the paper. "But let's get to the more important data—her personal statistics. Right here at the top of the first page. 'Place of birth: Augsburg. Date of birth: 25 February 1916. Parents: deceased. Brothers and sisters: none.' "

Koenig closed the file and passed it across the top of his desk. "You said I don't know the woman, Leutnant. I think perhaps I know her well enough."

Mueller took less than three minutes to read the file. It took much longer however for him to find his voice. "She did all that?"

"Falke is good at what she does. Including inventing a fictional life story to learn what she wants to know from young Luftwaffe pilots."

"How long have you had this? Before last night?"

"Yes, before last night. If you knew this information then, you might not have been able to play your role very well."

"The deaths of so many innocent people—women and children . . ."

And now, from the rear of the Me-110, she was

speaking to him. "Fritz, my man of iron—why are you so silent?"

Mueller's eyes narrowed. "I am silent only because I know what lies ahead for us," he said. "Especially what lies ahead for you."

From the back seat of the lead Me-110, Richter said, "You don't know yet, Major, the Countess may have escaped."

Koenig's response was slow in coming.

"Talking about it won't help, Hauptmann." Once more, the Major envisioned the explosion, the flaming Volkswagen. Again and again it burned, and Simone was gone. His many radioed inquiries to the maquis last night and just before they took off at dawn had produced no information about whether she lived or died. If indeed she had survived, the wheelchair might no longer be a false disguise.

"No, it doesn't help to talk," Richter replied, and felt almost unfair in thinking about the turn his own life had taken. His love for Elsa—for Ginny Cabot—was a glory within the broader tragedy. He wondered whether his ability as an intelligence agent would be compromised now. Would Elsa distract him with her love? Could they still be objective now?

He looked again at the boxes of diamonds strapped down beside Koenig's seat. He thought of Simone. 'Priceless,' Colonel Standish had said about these stones, but he was wrong. A price had been paid for them—a high price. He was trying to think of a way to console Koenig when von Spiegel's voice crackled in his ears:

"Company. Two birds. Seven o'clock and high."

The two British Spitfires nosed down and spread out.

"They're broadcasting something, Jack," one of the pilots said with a strong north-of-England roughness to his voice. "Sounds like English to me."

"Could be," came the answer. "Maybe something from the Book of Common Prayer. They're going to need it."

The twin-engined 110s were sitting ducks in any aerial combat with the faster and more maneuverable Spitfires. The Me-109 trailing the two ducks was more formidable in the skies, but once the 110s were downed, the odds would be in favor of His Majesty's royal duo.

"Second Hun on first pass, got it?"

"Right. I'm over, you're under."

"And never the twain shall meet. Try to remember that, Tony."

Renate Haas's eyes were wide, her brain confused because of what her ears had heard over the intercom. "What is happening—what is going on?"

"Quiet!" Mueller spat out. "We're in trouble!"

"But Major Koenig is speaking English!"

"I said shut up!"

Mueller had no doubt in his mind about what was being set up. The two Spitfires were singling him out for target number one. Meanwhile he could hear Koenig's voice speaking English: "Nightingale—I repeat, this is Nightingale! Goddammit, this is Nightingale! Do you hear me?"

Von Spiegel's voice, now also in English: "If they do, they're ignoring it. We've got no choice, John—you better get the hell out of here."

"Mueller," Koenig ordered, "take care of yourself!"

"I'll do what I can," Mueller answered. "You've got the goods, Major. Get them through."

Then Falke: "What are you talking about?"

Mueller ignored her. He could see von Spiegel's 109 coming down from eleven o'clock—coming fast. But it wasn't going to be fast enough. The two Spits were splitting their fields of fire, one coming in at nine o'clock, the other now pulling out of its dive so that it would be under Mueller's belly. He looked ahead and saw Koenig's plane with the diamonds dive toward the refuge of clouds. The diamonds. The mission. Right! That came first. It was up to him to save his own plane. The hell with the plane! It was up to him to save something more precious. The plane, after all, was Kraut—his skin was Australian. "Hold on," he said to nobody in particular, and pulled hard on the stick —all the way back.

The 110's nose instantly veered upward, and the fighter began to loop up into a tight circle. At the top of the circle, the plane dropped and the aircraft headed straight down like an arrow loosed from the heavens toward the unsuspecting earth below. His earphones told him that Renate Haas was screaming, but forget that! The main thing was to shake those Spitfires or, at the very least, keep them off-guard until von Spiegel could help out.

But even before he had pulled out of his dive, the first of the Spitfire machine gun messages smacked into the body of the 110. As he again leveled the plane, he saw that both Spits had followed him down—and they still had him in a crossfire. The 110 was a zombie—walking dead. The pilots of the Spits knew it, and the Australian knew it. It was only a matter of seconds now, and not many seconds.

The Perspex canopy over the cockpit in a 110 was constructed in three sections, the top section hinging aft and the two side sections folding downward. The Australian worked quickly and twisted the portside section free. As he did so he heard the woman behind him scream. She'd been screaming for some time now.

She was rigid, her eyes insanely wide, her small hands clenched in tight fists at the sides of her head. She had made a tangled mess of her parachute. He pulled himself upward and to port, making sure that his own chute was free. He stopped his movement, and then her screaming suddenly halted. For an instant her eyes cleared and found his.

"Please," she said. Just the one word, which he saw on her lips. Just the one word, imploring, and in English.

"I—" he began. That's as far as he got when the canopy of the 110 split into fragments in a chattering hail of machine gun fire. He had one glimpse of the lifeless, once beautiful face of Renate Haas. Then the face and the 110 were gone, and Mueller was falling free through empty space.

The RAF pilot named Tony radioed to his partner. "Watch it above you. The 109 is coming in!"

"I see him. Let's play, Tony."

"Damn you!" came an English voice that was from neither of the two Spitfires. "*Nightingale*—this is *Nightingale*! Does that mean anything to you lunkheads?"

"Tony—"

"I heard him, Jack—pull back. I'll talk. Messerschmitt. Repeat your message."

"Look at my underwings, limey! Double crosses! I'm Nightingale!"

The 109 banked and showed its underbelly to both Spits. "Did you see? Do you understand? You Geordie twit!"

The "Geordie"—north-of-England—pilot named Tony swallowed. "The other?"

"Nightingale, too."

"Check him, Jack."

"Right." Jack's Spit nosed down to follow the line of smoke that indicated the downward trail of the 110. It caught up to the other two fighters a few minutes later. "Flower blooming," the pilot reported.

"Only one chute?"

"Only one. Alive and kicking."

"Male?"

"Of course. What did you expect?"

After a pause, von Spiegel said, "Falcons have been known to fly. Now, if you boys will help me catch up to my leader, you will have my undying appreciation—and if you're lucky you won't be grounded permanently for the blunder you just made!"

"Don't ask," Colonel Freddy Standish said. His words were directed to Richter, who waited patiently until the bottle of Jim Beam, complete with glass, appeared on the desktop.

"I'll drink with the Hauptmann," said Oberleutnant von Spiegel.

"Might as well forget the coffee altogether," Major Koenig said. "I'll join you myself."

The Colonel placed two more glasses on the desk. Then he paused, nodded to himself, pulled a fourth from his desk drawer, and poured generously. They held up their glasses, and Standish said, "We're in your debt, John."

Koenig sipped the bourbon slowly. "You are in debt to others as well."

Standish drank and placed his glass on the desk. "We know that. And now sit down. I'm going to let you three in on a highly confidential secret that shall show you just how valuable those industrial diamonds are to us." He sipped the bourbon again and pursed his lips. "On Saturday, Hitler shall throw everything he's got at Russia."

The pilots sat, unmoving, stunned by the news.

"He's crazy!" von Spiegel said for all of them.

Standish said, "No one has suggested Hitler has been anything but crazy. But we're grateful for that madness now because that means Britain has been given the time we need to strengthen ourselves and eventually go on the offense. Hitler intends to commit sixty to seventy percent of his Luftwaffe to this stupid gamble, attacking Russia. It's all so secret that even Goering's Double Cross Staffel was kept in the dark. But in five days, the entire Russian frontier shall go up in flames."

"That gives you time, Colonel," Koenig said. "Use those industrial diamonds well."

"We shall," Standish said and poured another round of bourbon. The pilots were quiet, and Standish noticed that Koenig was particularly gloomy. "Is there something wrong, John?"

Koenig said nothing. Richter spoke up. "We had a rough night last night, Colonel. Some people important to us may have been lost."

"Oh," Standish said and stood. There was something about his eyes, thought Richter, something he had never seen there before. Standish was a hard number, always had been. Why, then, was there this twinkle in his eyes?

"If you're so depressed, John, then I suppose you wouldn't be interested in a dinner invitation tonight."

"That's right," Koenig said, and finished his bourbon. Then he looked at the Military Intelligence Colonel with a trace of curiosity.

"All right, John, I'll cancel on your behalf. I can understand your reluctance to be puttering about with countesses and such at a time like this. . . ."

Koenig was on his feet, hands flat on the desk. "Countesses?"

"Well, only one countess, actually, but I suppose one would be enough. The invitation came from Elsa Dietrich, who relayed a message she received early today and asked to pass it on to you. But, of course, I understand that such personal matters are out of place here. . . ."

"She's alive!" Koenig grabbed Standish by the shirt front. Standish drew away.

"If you're referring to a certain Countess Wilhelmina von Coburg, I suppose she must be alive. The message said she was in an automobile accident. Ran her car smack into a ditch, apparently. But friends were on hand in time to give her a lift home. She said dinner is at six sharp."

"We leave immediately!" Koenig said, and the other two pilots were on their feet. "Nightingale's going home, Colonel, or must I request permission?"

"Permission granted, John. By the way . . ."

Koenig stopped at the door.

"Don't take any unnecessary chances. If you and the Countess go out tonight, you do the driving, eh?"

Join the Allies on the Road to Victory
BANTAM WAR BOOKS

These action-packed books recount the most important events of World War II. Specially commissioned maps, diagrams and illustrations allow you to follow these true stories of brave men and gallantry in action.

Join the Allies on the Road to Victory
BANTAM WAR BOOKS

These action-packed books recount the most important events of World War II. Specially commissioned maps, diagrams and illustrations allow you to follow these true stories of brave men and gallantry in action.